ArtScroll Youth Series®

Rabbi Nosson Scherman / Rabbi Meir Zlotowitz

General Editors

Published by

Mesorah Publications, ltd

ARTSCROLL
YOUTH MEGILLAH

New simplified translation and comments by
Rabbi Nosson Scherman with Rabbi Meir Zlotowitz

Illustrated by
Michael Horen

Co-edited by
Rabbi Avie Gold

Designed by
Rabbi Sheah Brander

This Megillah is dedicated
to the memory of

Rabbi Meir Levi ז"ל
כ"ד חשון תשכ"ט
Rebbetzin Shoshana Levi ע"ה
י"ג כסלו תשל"ט

*Pioneers and molders of girls' chinuch in America,
they founded, led, taught — and set sterling personal examples —
in the Bais Yaakov of Brownsville, East New York, and Crown Heights.*

*By creating Camp Hedvah, they showed how much
an intelligently crafted summer can enrich a girl's life.*

*Their tradition lives on in Bais Yaakov d'Rav Meir and Camp Hedvah
where their legacy of* ודבר שלום לכל זרעו *continues to thrive in their children.*

תנצב"ה

FIRST EDITION
Thirteen Impressions . . . January 1988 — November 2019

Published and Distributed by
MESORAH PUBLICATIONS, Ltd.
4401 Second Avenue / Brooklyn, New York 11232

Distributed in Europe by
LEHMANNS
Unit E, Viking Business Park
Rolling Mill Road
Jarrow, Tyne & Wear NE32 3DP
England

Distributed in Australia & New Zealand by
GOLDS WORLD OF JUDAICA
3-13 William Street
Balaclava, Melbourne 3183
Victoria Australia

Distributed in Israel by
SIFRIATI / A. GITLER — BOOKS
POB 2351
Bnei Brak 51122

Distributed in South Africa by
KOLLEL BOOKSHOP
Northfield Centre 17 Northfield Avenue
Glenhazel 2192, Johannesburg, South Africa

ARTSCROLL® MESORAH SERIES
YOUTH MEGILLAH
© *Copyright 1988, 1993 by* MESORAH PUBLICATIONS, Ltd.
4401 Second Avenue / Brooklyn, N.Y. 11232 / (718) 921-9000/ www.artscroll.com

ISBN 10: 0-89906-067-6 / ISBN 13: 978-0-89906-067-5 (hard cover)
ISBN 10: 0-89906-068-4 / ISBN 13: 978-0-89906-068-2 (paperback)

Typography by CompuScribe at ArtScroll Studios, Ltd.
Printed in PRC

An Overview — A New Kind of Miracle

he Torah is filled with miracles. We always know that they were done by *Hashem*, because there was no other way that they could happen. Could *people* split the יַם סוּף, *Sea of Reeds*? Could *people* change sand to lice or kill every firstborn person and animal exactly at midnight? Could *people* stop the sun?

Of course not! Only *Hashem* could make such things happen.

But there are different kinds of miracles, too. Is it a miracle when we open our eyes in the morning after a good night's sleep, yawn, stretch, open our eyes and get ready for another day? Most people would say it is not a miracle, because the same thing happens to millions and millions of people every single day.

The truth is that miracles happen all the time, but we don't know they are miracles. Sometimes we don't know because they happen all the time, and sometimes we don't know because people seem to be doing everything on their own without *Hashem* changing the laws of nature. The *Megillah* shows us that when *Hashem* wants to help the Jewish people, He can do miracles in ways that seem to be absolutely normal. Let us look at some of the events in the *Megillah* and see how this happened. This is very important in Jewish history, because our חֲכָמִים, Sages, teach us that from the time of Mordechai and Esther, *Hashem* does miracles for us in a hidden way.

In the third year of King Achashveirosh's reign, the King made a very great party. Mordechai told the Jewish people not to take part in the feast, but they did not listen to him. They thought that it would be very dangerous to make the King angry with them. If the Jews would not go to his party, Achashveirosh might think they were not loyal to him!

Then, nine years later, Mordechai did something else that surprised his people. The King's new chief officer was Haman — and he wanted everyone to bow to him. It is true that Haman was a very bad person, but if the law was that everyone had to bow, there was no choice, was there? Yet Mordechai refused to bow. That made Haman so angry that he made the terrible plan to kill every single Jewish man, woman, and child! Whose fault was it? Mordechai's, of course! That is how it must have seemed to every sensible person. Then *Hashem* began to show us that 'sensible people' can make very foolish mistakes.

❀ ❀ ❀

The story is filled with parts that seem to have nothing to do with each other. And then, when it was all over, all the parts came together, like a jig-saw puzzle.

(1) At the end of Achashveirosh's great feast Queen Vashti was killed. She was punished because she did not obey the King's order. The one who advised the King to kill Vashti was a man named Memuchan. Our Sages tell us that Memuchan was another name for Haman. Thanks to the death of Vashti, Achashveirosh needed a new Queen. The woman he chose was Esther. As *we* know — but neither Achashveirosh nor Haman knew — she was Jewish. So it was because of Haman that a righteous Jewess became Queen of the world's greatest empire.

(2) Bigsan and Teresh were royal servants who plotted to kill the King. Because Queen Esther had asked the King to make Mordechai an official of the royal court, Mordechai was able to overhear Bigsan and Teresh. Mordechai told Esther about the danger to the King. She repeated the plot to Achashveirosh and told him that he owed his life to the loyal Mordechai. The King ordered that Mordechai's deed should be written in the royal record book. Then, everyone forgot all about it — until the time came to save the Jewish people.

(3) Mordechai refused to bow to Haman. Soon after that, Esther let it be known that, to her, Haman was nearly as important as the King himself: she invited the King and Haman — and no one else — to a special drinking party. Haman was so proud! And he was so sure of his importance that he built a gallows to hang Mordechai on. Then, happy and proud of himself, he came to Achashveirosh to get permission for the hanging. What a surprise awaited him!

❀ ❀ ❀

When we read the story of the *Megillah,* we see how all of these separate sets of events came together to save the Jewish people. Haman, was a grandchild of Amalek, and he wanted to carry out his ancestor's goal of destroying the Jewish people — yet Haman was the one who made it possible for them to be saved. Esther became Queen because of him, and he was hung on the gallows that he himself had built for Mordechai. On the same night when Haman was ready to murder Mordechai, Achashveirosh remembered that Mordechai had saved the King's life. Not

only did he reward Mordechai with great honors, but he must have begun thinking that perhaps Mordechai, not Haman, was his most loyal servant.

And the Jewish people? Finally, nine years after the King's feast, the Jews realized that Mordechai had been right all along: they should *not* have taken part in the feast and Mordechai did the right thing in not bowing to Haman.

Was this a miracle? It was.

❊ ❊ ❊

Hashem's Name is not found in the entire *Megillah;* it is the only book of the Torah where we do not find His Holy Name. That is because Mordechai and Esther, who wrote the *Megillah,* wanted to show us that *Hashem* is always present, even when we cannot tell. Someone could read *Megillas Esther* as if it were just a very interesting story that is filled with surprises, but that would be a mistake. Mordechai and Esther knew the truth. *Hashem* revealed to them that the different events of the story did not come together by accident. It was *Hashem* Who made everything happen that way.

The story of Purim is still important to us. It took place in the years after the First *Beis Hamikdash* was destroyed and the Jewish people were spread out in the foreign lands of exile. Before long we wouldn't have prophets anymore to bring us messages from *Hashem.* People wondered if *Hashem* would still care about us. The *Megillah* tells us that the answer is yes. Miracles will still happen, even though we may never know. And the Jewish people will always survive, as long as we have faith in *Hashem* and in righteous leaders like Mordechai and Esther.

The Reason for the Feast

he feast of Achashveirosh is very important to the story of Purim. It lasted for more than six months. We can imagine how much money it must have cost to make such a feast. What was the King celebrating that was worth so much time and money?

The story of Purim happened after the Jewish people were sent into גָּלוּת, *exile,* and the *Beish Hamikdash* was destroyed. Those terrible things didn't happen all at once. First King Nevuchadnetzar of Babylonia conquered *Eretz Yisrael.* Eight years after that, he took King Yechaniah and the great Torah scholars from Jerusalem and forced them to go to Babylonia. That was the first part of the exile. After another eleven years, Nevuchadnetzar destroyed the *Beis Hamikdash* and forced most of the Jewish people to leave the country.

The prophet Yirmiyahu had said that the exile would last for only seventy years, and then the Jewish people would be able to build a new *Beis Hamikdash* and go back to *Eretz Yisrael.*

The kings of Babylonia and Persia were afraid of that. They all knew that under King David and King Shlomo *Eretz Yisrael* had been the center of the world. They knew of the miracles that *Hashem* had done for the Jewish people since they left Egypt. If a new *Beis Hamikdash* was to be built, as Yirmiyahu had said, that might mean that Israel would become a great power once again. That was a thought that frightened the kings of that part of the world.

But they were hoping that Yirmiyahu's prophecy would not come true. They thought that if the Jews did not deserve it, *Hashem* would forget about them and they would never again go back to their land. How could the kings know if the Jews would lose their chance to go back to *Eretz Yisrael?* They would wait for the end of the seventy years. If that time passed and the Jews remained in exile, it would mean that they would never again be an important nation.

Achashveirosh thought that the exile should be counted from the year that Yechaniah and the Torah scholars were forced to leave the country. If the Jews did not have their true King and they did not have their Torah leaders, they had to be considered like a nation in exile, even if they still lived in *Eretz Yisrael.* When seventy years passed from that time and the Jews were still in exile, Achashveirosh was overjoyed. To celebrate, he made the great, great feast that the *Megillah* begins with.

He was wrong. *Hashem* was counting the seventy years from the destruction of the *Beis Hamikdash.* When seventy years passed from that time, Achashveirosh was no longer alive. The new King was Darius, the son of Achashveirosh and Esther. He gave the Jews permission to build the Second *Beis Hamikdash* (*Megillah* 11b; *Otzar Ha'Iggeres*).

Laws of Purim

מַחֲצִית הַשֶּׁקֶל / Half a Shekel

Before the *Megillah* is read on the evening of Purim, it is customary for everyone to give a contribution of מַחֲצִית הַשֶּׁקֶל, *half a shekel*. In each country, the custom is to give half of the generally accepted coin, or denomination of money. Thus, in the United States, one gives half a dollar, in England, half a pound, and so on. Since the Jews in the Wilderness gave three such contributions when the מִשְׁכָּן, *Tabernacle,* was built, we give three half-*shekels*. This money is distributed to the poor.

מִקְרָא מְגִלָּה / The Megillah Reading

Every man and woman must hear the *Megillah* two times, once in the evening of Purim and once during the day. It is preferable to hear the *Megillah* in the synagogue, but if one cannot do so, it may be read at home. In honor of the *Megillah,* people should dress in their Sabbath clothing.

The listeners must hear every word of the *Megillah.* Because of this, the reader should be very careful not to read when it is noisy or when the children are making noise after hearing the name of Haman. For the same reason, parents should control their children's noise-making, and should not bring children who are too young to remain quiet.

It is forbidden to speak from the time the reader starts the blessings until after the blessing following the *Megillah.*

עַל הַנִּסִּים / Al Hanissim

During *Shemoneh Esrei* and *Bircas Hamazon,* we recite עַל הַנִּסִּים, *For the miracles.* However, if one has forgotten to recite this prayer he is not required to repeat *Shemoneh Esrei* or *Bircas Hamazon.*

מִצְוֹת הַיּוֹם / Three Additional Mitzvos

During the day of Purim there are three additional *mitzvos:* מִשְׁלוֹחַ מָנוֹת, *Gifts of food to friends;* מַתָּנוֹת לָאֶבְיוֹנִים, *Gifts to the poor;* and סְעוּדַת פּוּרִים, the *Purim Feast.*

מִשְׁלוֹחַ מָנוֹת / Mishloach Manos / Gifts of Food

Every man and woman is required to send a gift to at least one fellow Jew. The gift must consist of at least two ready-to-eat foods, either raw or prepared. Every member of the family should be careful to send his or her own gift, and not rely on those sent by the heads of the family.

One may make these gifts as large as he likes and may send gifts to as many people as he likes. However, it is much better to allocate one's time, funds, and energy toward gifts for the poor than toward gifts for one's friends.

מַתָּנוֹת לָאֶבְיוֹנִים / Matanos La'evyonim / Gifts to the Poor

Everyone is required to give gifts to at least two poor people. In order that the poor person be able to enjoy these gifts on Purim, they should consist of food or money.

Nothing makes God happier than bringing happiness to the poor, the widowed, and the orphaned. Therefore, we should be as generous as possible in our gifts to the poor.

סְעוּדַת פּוּרִים / The Purim Feast

It is a *mitzvah* to eat, drink, and rejoice on Purim. Although one should have a larger and better meal than usual after the evening *Megillah* reading, the true *mitzvah* of the Purim feast is during the day, because the *Megillah* speaks of יְמֵי שִׂמְחָה, *days of celebration*.

The feast should be celebrated after *Minchah*. Since it is one of the *mitzvos* of Purim day, one must begin it while it is still daytime, and should eat most of it before evening. Therefore, the time-consuming preparation and delivery of *mishloach manos* and *matanos la'evyonim* should not be permitted to delay the Purim feast too late in the day.

It is praiseworthy to devote some time to Torah study before the feast, because the miracle of Purim involved the study of, and a new love for the Torah.

If Purim falls on a Friday, the feast should be held early in the day so that one will have an appetite for the Sabbath feast that evening.

❧BLESSINGS BEFORE THE MEGILLAH READING / בְּרָכוֹת לִפְנֵי קְרִיאַת הַמְּגִלָּה❧

Before reading the *Megillah* on Purim, the reader recites the following three blessings out loud. Everyone should answer only אָמֵן, *Amen,* but not בָּרוּךְ הוּא וּבָרוּךְ שְׁמוֹ. When we listen to the blessings we must have in mind that the reader is reciting them for us, and we must listen to each word carefully. From the time the reader begins the first blessing until the end of the blessing after the *Megillah,* we are not allowed to talk. We should be careful to hear every word of the *Megillah.*

In the morning, the reader recites the same three blessings, but there is something special that we all should have in mind when we listen to the blessing of שֶׁהֶחֱיָנוּ. This blessing thanks *Hashem* for keeping us alive so that we can do a new *mitzvah;* therefore, we must think about the *new mitzvos* that we will be doing on Purim day. So on the morning of Purim, we should have in mind that later in the day we will be doing the *mitzvos* of giving *Shloach Manos* to our friends, giving gifts to poor people, and eating the Purim feast.

 e bless You, Hashem our God, King of the whole world, Who made us holy with His commandments, and commanded us about the mitzvah of reading the Megillah.

(All— *Amen* .)

בָּרוּךְ אַתָּה יהוה אֱלֹהֵינוּ מֶלֶךְ הָעוֹלָם, אֲשֶׁר קִדְּשָׁנוּ בְּמִצְוֹתָיו, וְצִוָּנוּ עַל מִקְרָא מְגִלָּה. (אָמֵן. —All)

 e bless you, Hashem our God, King of the whole world, Who made miracles for our forefathers, in those days at this time of the year. (All— *Amen.*)

בָּרוּךְ אַתָּה יהוה אֱלֹהֵינוּ מֶלֶךְ הָעוֹלָם, שֶׁעָשָׂה נִסִּים לַאֲבוֹתֵינוּ, בַּיָּמִים הָהֵם, בַּזְּמַן הַזֶּה. (אָמֵן. —All)

 e bless you, Hashem our God, King of the whole world, for keeping us alive, taking care of us, and bringing us to this season. (All— *Amen.*)

בָּרוּךְ אַתָּה יהוה אֱלֹהֵינוּ מֶלֶךְ הָעוֹלָם, שֶׁהֶחֱיָנוּ, וְקִיְּמָנוּ, וְהִגִּיעָנוּ לַזְּמַן הַזֶּה. (אָמֵן. —All)

Note: During the reading of the Megillah, four verses are recited out loud by the congregation and then they are read by the reader. These four verses — 2:5 (p. 14), 8:15 and 8:16 (p. 40), and 10:3 (p. 45) — are shown in bold type and in color in this Megillah.

Achashveirosh, the King of Persia and Media, made a big party in his palace garden.
He let the people use his best furniture and gave them lots of wine to drink.

א – 1

his happened in the days of Achashveirosh — who was King of a hundred and twenty-seven countries, from Hodu to Cush. [2]In those days, King Achashveirosh sat on his royal throne in Shushan the Capital. [3]In the third year after he became King, he make a feast for all his officers and his servants; the army of Persia and Media, the nobles and the officers of the countries were there. [4]For a long time — for a hundred and eighty days — he showed off the rich treasures of his kingdom and the beauty and greatness of his rule.

[5]And when these days ended, the King made a week-long party for everyone in Shushan the Capital, for the great people and the plain people, in the garden of the King's palace. [6]There were drapes of fine white cotton and blue wool, held with cords of fine linen and purple wool, on silver rods and marble pillars; there were gold and silver couches, and the floor was made of green and white precious marble. [7]The drinks were served in golden cups — no two cups were alike — and there was a lot of royal wine, as only a King could afford. [8]And the drinks were served according to this rule: "No one should be forced." They did that because the King had ordered all his officials to do what every guest wanted.

וַיְהִי בִּימֵי אֲחַשְׁוֵרוֹשׁ הוּא אֲחַשְׁוֵרוֹשׁ הַמֹּלֵךְ מֵהֹדּוּ וְעַד־כּוּשׁ שֶׁבַע וְעֶשְׂרִים וּמֵאָה מְדִינָה: ב בַּיָּמִים הָהֵם כְּשֶׁבֶת ו הַמֶּלֶךְ אֲחַשְׁוֵרוֹשׁ עַל כִּסֵּא מַלְכוּתוֹ אֲשֶׁר בְּשׁוּשַׁן הַבִּירָה: ג בִּשְׁנַת שָׁלוֹשׁ לְמָלְכוֹ עָשָׂה מִשְׁתֶּה לְכָל־שָׂרָיו וַעֲבָדָיו חֵיל ו פָּרַס וּמָדַי הַפַּרְתְּמִים וְשָׂרֵי הַמְּדִינוֹת לְפָנָיו: ד בְּהַרְאֹתוֹ אֶת־עֹשֶׁר כְּבוֹד מַלְכוּתוֹ וְאֶת־יְקָר תִּפְאֶרֶת גְּדוּלָּתוֹ יָמִים רַבִּים שְׁמוֹנִים וּמְאַת יוֹם: ה וּבִמְלוֹאת ו הַיָּמִים הָאֵלֶּה עָשָׂה הַמֶּלֶךְ לְכָל־הָעָם הַנִּמְצְאִים בְּשׁוּשַׁן הַבִּירָה לְמִגָּדוֹל וְעַד־קָטָן מִשְׁתֶּה שִׁבְעַת יָמִים בַּחֲצַר גִּנַּת בִּיתַן הַמֶּלֶךְ: ו חוּר ו כַּרְפַּס וּתְכֵלֶת אָחוּז בְּחַבְלֵי־בוּץ וְאַרְגָּמָן עַל־גְּלִילֵי כֶסֶף וְעַמּוּדֵי שֵׁשׁ מִטּוֹת ו זָהָב וָכֶסֶף עַל רִצְפַת בַּהַט־וָשֵׁשׁ וְדַר וְסֹחָרֶת: ז וְהַשְׁקוֹת בִּכְלֵי זָהָב וְכֵלִים מִכֵּלִים שׁוֹנִים וְיַיִן מַלְכוּת רָב כְּיַד הַמֶּלֶךְ: ח וְהַשְׁתִיָּה כַדָּת אֵין אֹנֵס כִּי־כֵן ו יִסַּד הַמֶּלֶךְ עַל כָּל־רַב בֵּיתוֹ לַעֲשׂוֹת כִּרְצוֹן אִישׁ־וָאִישׁ:

Hashem remembers. Once, Rabbi Akiva noticed that his students were falling asleep. In order to get their attention, he asked: "Why did Esther deserve to become the Queen of 127 countries? Because *Hashem* said, 'Let the daughter of Sarah who lived 127 years [and was righteous all of that time] come and be the Queen of 127 countries' " (*Midrash*).

The Jewish Sin. At the feast, everyone drank from golden cups. Even the beautiful cups that the Babylonians had stolen from the *Beis Hamikdash* were brought in. Mordechai told the Jews not to join in the feast, but they didn't listen to him. They went and enjoyed themselves. So *Hashem* punished them by letting Haman try to kill them (*Megillah* 12a).

The King sent servants to bring Queen Vashti.
He wanted to show all the people how beautiful she was. But she said, "NO!"

 Queen Vashti also made a feast for the women in the palace of King Achashveirosh.

[10] On the seventh day, when the King was a little drunk, he spoke to Mehuman, Bizesa, Charvonah, Bigesa, Abagesa, Zeisar, and Carcas, who were the seven main servants of King Achashveirosh. — [11]He ordered them to bring Queen Vashti to him wearing her royal crown, to show off her beauty to the people and the officers, for she was very beautiful. [12]But Queen Vashti refused to obey the order that

גַּם וַשְׁתִּי הַמַּלְכָּה עָשְׂתָה מִשְׁתֵּה נָשִׁים בֵּית הַמַּלְכוּת אֲשֶׁר לַמֶּלֶךְ אֲחַשְׁוֵרוֹשׁ: י בַּיּוֹם הַשְּׁבִיעִי כְּטוֹב לֵב־הַמֶּלֶךְ בַּיָּיִן אָמַר לִמְהוּמָן בִּזְּתָא חַרְבוֹנָא בִּגְתָא וַאֲבַגְתָא זֵתַר וְכַרְכַּס שִׁבְעַת הַסָּרִיסִים הַמְשָׁרְתִים אֶת־ פְּנֵי הַמֶּלֶךְ אֲחַשְׁוֵרוֹשׁ: יא לְהָבִיא אֶת־וַשְׁתִּי הַמַּלְכָּה לִפְנֵי הַמֶּלֶךְ בְּכֶתֶר מַלְכוּת לְהַרְאוֹת הָעַמִּים וְהַשָּׂרִים אֶת־יָפְיָהּ כִּי־טוֹבַת מַרְאֶה הִיא: יב וַתְּמָאֵן הַמַּלְכָּה וַשְׁתִּי לָבוֹא בִּדְבַר

the King had sent with the servants. The King became very furious; he was burning with anger.
[13]Then the King spoke with his wise men, for the King used to discuss problems with people who knew the rules and the laws. [14]The wise men closest to him were Carshena, Shesar, Admasa, Tarshish, Meres, Marsena and Memuchan, who were the seven officers of Persia and Media who were always allowed to see the King, and who were the highest officers in the kingdom. [15]King Achashveirosh

הַמֶּ֫לֶךְ אֲשֶׁר בְּיַד הַסָּרִיסִים וַיִּקְצֹף הַמֶּ֫לֶךְ
מְאֹד וַחֲמָתוֹ בָּעֲרָה בוֹ:
יג וַיֹּ֫אמֶר הַמֶּ֫לֶךְ לַחֲכָמִים יֹדְעֵי הָעִתִּים
כִּי־כֵן דְּבַר הַמֶּ֫לֶךְ לִפְנֵי כָּל־יֹדְעֵי דָּת וָדִין:
יד וְהַקָּרֹב אֵלָיו כַּרְשְׁנָא שֵׁתָר אַדְמָ֫תָא
תַּרְשִׁישׁ מֶ֫רֶס מַרְסְנָא מְמוּכָן שִׁבְעַת שָׂרֵי |
פָּרַס וּמָדַי רֹאֵי פְּנֵי הַמֶּ֫לֶךְ הַיֹּשְׁבִים רִאשֹׁנָה

Vashti's Punishment. Queen Vashti hated the Jewish people. She used to take Jewish girls and make them work for her on *Shabbos*. That is why *Hashem* punished her on *Shabbos*, which was the seventh day of Achashveirosh's feast. When the King sent for her, *Hashem* made a sickness break out all over her skin. That is why she refused to go to the King. Achashveirosh didn't know that. He became so angry that he had her killed (*Megillah* 12b).

wanted them to tell him the right way to punish Queen Vashti for not obeying the order that he had sent with the servants.

[16]Memuchan spoke up before the King and the officers:

Queen Vashti has done wrong not only to the King, but also to all the officers and all the people in all the countries of King Achashveirosh. [17]For all the women will find out what the Queen did, and they will insult their own husbands. They will say, "Even King Achashveirosh ordered Queen Vashti to be brought to him, and she did not come!" [18]As soon as the princesses of Persia and Media hear what the Queen did they will talk the same way to all the King's officers, and there will be much insult and anger.

[19]If the King likes this idea, let him issue a royal decree, and let it be written into the law books of Persia and Media, so that it cannot be changed: that Vashti will never again come to King Achashveirosh; and let the King give her place as Queen to someone who is better than she is. [20]When the King's new decree will be heard all over his kingdom — even though the kingdom is so large — then all the wives will show respect to their husbands, great and plain alike.

[21]The King and the officers liked this idea, and the King did as Memuchan said. [22]He sent letters to all the King's countries, to each country in its own script and to each nation in its own language, ordering that every man should be the master in his own home, and the whole family should speak the language of his people.

בַּמַּלְכוּת: טו כְּדָת מַה־לַּעֲשׂוֹת בַּמַּלְכָּה וַשְׁתִּי עַל | אֲשֶׁר לֹא־עָשְׂתָה אֶת־מַאֲמַר הַמֶּלֶךְ אֲחַשְׁוֵרוֹשׁ בְּיַד הַסָּרִיסִים: טז וַיֹּאמֶר מְמוּכָן לִפְנֵי הַמֶּלֶךְ וְהַשָּׂרִים לֹא עַל־הַמֶּלֶךְ לְבַדּוֹ עָוְתָה וַשְׁתִּי הַמַּלְכָּה כִּי עַל־כָּל־הַשָּׂרִים וְעַל־כָּל־הָעַמִּים אֲשֶׁר בְּכָל־מְדִינוֹת הַמֶּלֶךְ אֲחַשְׁוֵרוֹשׁ: יז כִּי־יֵצֵא דְבַר־הַמַּלְכָּה עַל־כָּל־הַנָּשִׁים לְהַבְזוֹת בַּעְלֵיהֶן בְּעֵינֵיהֶן בְּאָמְרָם הַמֶּלֶךְ אֲחַשְׁוֵרוֹשׁ אָמַר לְהָבִיא אֶת־וַשְׁתִּי הַמַּלְכָּה לְפָנָיו וְלֹא־בָאָה: יח וְהַיּוֹם הַזֶּה תֹּאמַרְנָה | שָׂרוֹת פָּרַס־וּמָדַי אֲשֶׁר שָׁמְעוּ אֶת־דְּבַר הַמַּלְכָּה לְכֹל שָׂרֵי הַמֶּלֶךְ וּכְדַי בִּזָּיוֹן וָקָצֶף: יט אִם־עַל־הַמֶּלֶךְ טוֹב יֵצֵא דְבַר־מַלְכוּת מִלְּפָנָיו וְיִכָּתֵב בְּדָתֵי פָרַס־וּמָדַי וְלֹא יַעֲבוֹר אֲשֶׁר לֹא־תָבוֹא וַשְׁתִּי לִפְנֵי הַמֶּלֶךְ אֲחַשְׁוֵרוֹשׁ וּמַלְכוּתָהּ יִתֵּן הַמֶּלֶךְ לִרְעוּתָהּ הַטּוֹבָה מִמֶּנָּה: כ וְנִשְׁמַע פִּתְגָם הַמֶּלֶךְ אֲשֶׁר־יַעֲשֶׂה בְּכָל־מַלְכוּתוֹ כִּי רַבָּה הִיא וְכָל־הַנָּשִׁים יִתְּנוּ יְקָר לְבַעְלֵיהֶן לְמִגָּדוֹל וְעַד־קָטָן: כא וַיִּיטַב הַדָּבָר בְּעֵינֵי הַמֶּלֶךְ וְהַשָּׂרִים וַיַּעַשׂ הַמֶּלֶךְ כִּדְבַר מְמוּכָן: כב וַיִּשְׁלַח סְפָרִים אֶל־כָּל־מְדִינוֹת הַמֶּלֶךְ אֶל־מְדִינָה וּמְדִינָה כִּכְתָבָהּ וְאֶל־עַם וָעָם כִּלְשׁוֹנוֹ לִהְיוֹת כָּל־אִישׁ שֹׂרֵר בְּבֵיתוֹ וּמְדַבֵּר כִּלְשׁוֹן עַמּוֹ:

°מוֹמְכָן כ׳

Hashem's Plan. When *Hashem* wants to help us, He makes people do strange things. Achashveirosh tried very hard to make the men in his Kingdom feel very important. That is why he said that every husband should be the master of his own family. But the King wanted to embarrass his own wife in public, and when she refused, he had her killed! *Hashem* made this happen so that Esther would become the Queen and be able to save the Jewish people (*Vilna Gaon*).

ב – II

After all this happened, when the anger of King Achashveirosh calmed down, he remembered Vashti and what she had done, and how she had been punished. [2]Then the King's young servants said to him:

Let us try to find beautiful young girls for the King. [3]Let the King appoint agents in all the countries of his kingdom, to gather all the beautiful young girls and bring them to Shushan the Capital to the harem, under the care of Hegai, the King's servant who guards the women; and they should be given their cosmetics. [4]Then, the girl whom the King likes best should become Queen in place of Vashti.

The King liked this idea and he did so.

אַחַר הַדְּבָרִים הָאֵלֶּה כְּשֹׁךְ חֲמַת הַמֶּלֶךְ אֲחַשְׁוֵרוֹשׁ זָכַר אֶת־וַשְׁתִּי וְאֵת אֲשֶׁר־עָשָׂתָה וְאֵת אֲשֶׁר־נִגְזַר עָלֶיהָ: ב וַיֹּאמְרוּ נַעֲרֵי־הַמֶּלֶךְ מְשָׁרְתָיו יְבַקְשׁוּ לַמֶּלֶךְ נְעָרוֹת בְּתוּלוֹת טוֹבוֹת מַרְאֶה: ג וְיַפְקֵד הַמֶּלֶךְ פְּקִידִים בְּכָל־מְדִינוֹת מַלְכוּתוֹ וְיִקְבְּצוּ אֶת־כָּל־נַעֲרָה־בְתוּלָה טוֹבַת מַרְאֶה אֶל־שׁוּשַׁן הַבִּירָה אֶל־בֵּית הַנָּשִׁים אֶל־יַד הֵגֶא סְרִיס הַמֶּלֶךְ שֹׁמֵר הַנָּשִׁים וְנָתוֹן תַּמְרֻקֵיהֶן: ד וְהַנַּעֲרָה אֲשֶׁר תִּיטַב בְּעֵינֵי הַמֶּלֶךְ תִּמְלֹךְ תַּחַת וַשְׁתִּי וַיִּיטַב הַדָּבָר בְּעֵינֵי הַמֶּלֶךְ וַיַּעַשׂ כֵּן:

There was a Jewish man in Shushan the Capital whose name was Mordechai, son of Yair, son of Shimi, son of Kish, of the tribe of Benjamin. [6]He had been forced to leave Jerusalem along with the others who had been forced to leave with Yechaniah, King of Judah, whom Nevuchadnetzar, King of Babylon, had taken away. [7]Mordechai had raised Hadassah — who was also called Esther — his cousin; since she did not have a father or mother. The girl had fine features and she was beautiful; and when her father and mother had died, Mordechai adopted her as his daughter.

[8]When the King's order became known, many young girls were brought to Shushan the Capital, under the care of Hegai. Esther, too, was taken to the palace, under the care of Hegai, who guarded the women. [9]He liked the girl and he wanted to be nice to her; quickly he arranged for her cosmetics and her meals. He also gave her seven special maids from the royal palace; and he moved her and her maids to the best rooms in the harem. [10]Esther did not tell anyone what nation she was from or where she was born, for Mordechai had ordered her not to tell.

אִ֣ישׁ יְהוּדִ֔י הָיָ֖ה בְּשׁוּשַׁ֣ן הַבִּירָ֑ה וּשְׁמ֣וֹ מָרְדֳּכַ֗י בֶּ֣ן יָאִ֧יר בֶּן־שִׁמְעִ֛י בֶּן־קִ֖ישׁ אִ֥ישׁ יְמִינִֽי: ו אֲשֶׁ֤ר הׇגְלָה֙ מִירֽוּשָׁלַ֔יִם עִם־הַגֹּלָה֙ אֲשֶׁ֣ר הׇגְלְתָ֔ה עִ֚ם יְכׇנְיָ֣ה מֶֽלֶךְ־יְהוּדָ֔ה אֲשֶׁ֣ר הֶגְלָ֔ה נְבֽוּכַדְנֶאצַּ֖ר מֶ֥לֶךְ בָּבֶֽל: ז וַיְהִ֣י אֹמֵ֗ן אֶת־הֲדַסָּ֗ה הִ֤יא אֶסְתֵּר֙ בַּת־דֹּד֔וֹ כִּ֛י אֵ֥ין לָ֖הּ אָ֣ב וָאֵ֑ם וְהַנַּעֲרָ֤ה יְפַת־תֹּ֙אַר֙ וְטוֹבַ֣ת מַרְאֶ֔ה וּבְמ֤וֹת אָבִ֙יהָ֙ וְאִמָּ֔הּ לְקָחָ֧הּ מָרְדֳּכַ֛י ל֖וֹ לְבַֽת: ח וַיְהִ֗י בְּהִשָּׁמַ֤ע דְּבַר־הַמֶּ֙לֶךְ֙ וְדָת֔וֹ וּֽבְהִקָּבֵ֞ץ נְעָר֥וֹת רַבּ֛וֹת אֶל־שׁוּשַׁ֥ן הַבִּירָ֖ה אֶל־יַ֣ד הֵגָ֑י וַתִּלָּקַ֤ח אֶסְתֵּר֙ אֶל־בֵּ֣ית הַמֶּ֔לֶךְ אֶל־יַ֥ד הֵגַ֖י שֹׁמֵ֥ר הַנָּשִֽׁים: ט וַתִּיטַ֨ב הַנַּעֲרָ֣ה בְעֵינָיו֮ וַתִּשָּׂ֣א חֶ֣סֶד לְפָנָיו֒ וַ֠יְבַהֵ֠ל אֶת־תַּמְרוּקֶ֤יהָ וְאֶת־מָנוֹתֶ֙הָ֙ לָתֵ֣ת לָ֔הּ וְאֵת֙ שֶׁ֣בַע הַנְּעָר֔וֹת הָרְאֻי֥וֹת לָֽתֶת־לָ֖הּ מִבֵּ֣ית הַמֶּ֑לֶךְ וַיְשַׁנֶּ֧הָ וְאֶת־נַעֲרוֹתֶ֛יהָ לְט֖וֹב בֵּ֥ית הַנָּשִֽׁים: י לֹא־הִגִּ֣ידָה אֶסְתֵּ֔ר אֶת־עַמָּ֖הּ וְאֶת־מֽוֹלַדְתָּ֑הּ כִּ֧י מׇרְדֳּכַ֛י צִוָּ֥ה עָלֶ֖יהָ אֲשֶׁ֥ר לֹֽא־תַגִּֽיד:

A Man from Benjamin. Mordechai and Esther, the ones who saved the Jews, came from the tribe of Benjamin. Why did Benjamin deserve this honor? Because Benjamin was the only one of the brothers who had nothing to do with selling Joseph (*Midrash*).

Esther's Secret. Mordechai was sure that Hashem wanted to use Esther to help the Jews. But if Achashveirosh knew she was Jewish, he would never have made her Queen. That is why Mordechai told her not to tell she was Jewish (*Rokeach*).

Seven Maids for Seven Days. Esther used her maids to help her keep the secret that she was Jewish. She had seven maids, a different one for each day of the week. That way, when the "seventh maid" came, Esther would know it was *Shabbos* (*Megillah* 13a).

If the maids had known that she rested on *Shabbos*, they would have guessed that she was Jewish. But she fooled them. The weekday maids always saw her working, and the *Shabbos* maid always saw her resting. That way, none of the maids knew that Esther rested only on *Shabbos* (*Yaaros D'vash*).

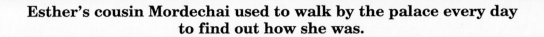

Esther's cousin Mordechai used to walk by the palace every day to find out how she was.

[11]Every day Mordechai used to walk in front of the courtyard of the harem to find out if Esther was well and what would happen to her.

יא וּבְכָל־י֣וֹם וָי֔וֹם מָרְדֳּכַי֙ מִתְהַלֵּ֔ךְ לִפְנֵ֖י חֲצַ֣ר בֵּית־הַנָּשִׁ֑ים לָדַ֙עַת֙ אֶת־שְׁל֣וֹם אֶסְתֵּ֔ר וּמַה־יֵּעָשֶׂ֖ה בָּֽהּ׃

15 / YOUTH MEGILLAH

For a whole year, the girls got perfumes and cosmetics. Every day a different girl would come to Achashveirosh, but he didn't like any of them for his Queen.

¹²Now each girl had her turn to come to King Achashveirosh, after she received beauty treatments for twelve months, because that was how long the treatments took: six months with oil of myrrh, and six months with perfumes and ladies' cosmetics. ¹³Then, when the girl was ready to come to the King, she was given anything she wanted to bring along from the harem to the palace. ¹⁴In the evening she would come, and in the morning she would be sent to the second harem under the care of Shaashgaz, the King's servant, who guarded the royal ladies. She was never again allowed to go to the King, unless the King wanted her, and then she would be called for by name.

יב וּבְהַגִּיעַ תֹּר נַעֲרָה וְנַעֲרָה לָבוֹא | אֶל־ הַמֶּלֶךְ אֲחַשְׁוֵרוֹשׁ מִקֵּץ הֱיוֹת לָהּ כְּדָת הַנָּשִׁים שְׁנֵים עָשָׂר חֹדֶשׁ כִּי כֵּן יִמְלְאוּ יְמֵי מְרוּקֵיהֶן שִׁשָּׁה חֳדָשִׁים בְּשֶׁמֶן הַמֹּר וְשִׁשָּׁה חֳדָשִׁים בַּבְּשָׂמִים וּבְתַמְרוּקֵי הַנָּשִׁים: יג וּבָזֶה הַנַּעֲרָה בָּאָה אֶל־הַמֶּלֶךְ אֵת כָּל־אֲשֶׁר תֹּאמַר יִנָּתֵן לָהּ לָבוֹא עִמָּהּ מִבֵּית הַנָּשִׁים עַד־בֵּית הַמֶּלֶךְ: יד בָּעֶרֶב | הִיא בָאָה וּבַבֹּקֶר הִיא שָׁבָה אֶל־בֵּית הַנָּשִׁים שֵׁנִי אֶל־ יַד שַׁעַשְׁגַז סְרִיס הַמֶּלֶךְ שֹׁמֵר הַפִּילַגְשִׁים לֹא־תָבוֹא עוֹד אֶל־הַמֶּלֶךְ כִּי אִם־חָפֵץ בָּהּ הַמֶּלֶךְ וְנִקְרְאָה בְשֵׁם:

hen it was the turn of Esther, daughter of Avichail the uncle of Mordechai (who had adopted her as his own daughter), to come to the King, she didn't ask for anything except for what was ordered for her by Hegai the King's servant who guarded the women. Everyone who saw Esther liked her.

¹⁶Esther was taken to King Achashveirosh in his palace in the tenth month, the month of Teves, in the seventh year after he became King. ¹⁷The King

וּבְהַגִּיעַ תֹּר־אֶסְתֵּר בַּת־אֲבִיחַיִל דֹּד מָרְדֳּכַי אֲשֶׁר לָקַח־לוֹ לְבַת לָבוֹא אֶל־הַמֶּלֶךְ לֹא בִקְשָׁה דָּבָר כִּי אִם אֶת־אֲשֶׁר יֹאמַר הֵגַי סְרִיס־הַמֶּלֶךְ שֹׁמֵר הַנָּשִׁים וַתְּהִי אֶסְתֵּר נֹשֵׂאת חֵן בְּעֵינֵי כָּל־רֹאֶיהָ: טו וַתִּלָּקַח אֶסְתֵּר אֶל־הַמֶּלֶךְ אֲחַשְׁוֵרוֹשׁ אֶל־בֵּית מַלְכוּתוֹ בַּחֹדֶשׁ הָעֲשִׂירִי הוּא־חֹדֶשׁ טֵבֵת בִּשְׁנַת־שֶׁבַע לְמַלְכוּתוֹ: טז וַיֶּאֱהַב הַמֶּלֶךְ

The Second Harem. Any girl who came to Achashveirosh was never allowed to marry anyone else, even if she was not picked to be Queen. All these girls went to live in a special palace called a harem. Every once in a while, the King might send for one of them (*Ibn Ezra*).

Esther's Family. This is the first time we are told who Esther's father was. Why was it not said before? And why does the Megillah repeat once again that she was Mordechai's relative?

Esther always remembered that her father had been a *tzaddik,* and that the one who raised her was Mordechai, her

relative and the leader of the Jewish people. Since she came from such a holy family, she did not want Achashveirosh or the people in the harem to like her. Therefore she never asked for perfume or cosmetics, hoping that they will not think that she is pretty, and they would send her home.

Who Is She? Achashveirosh wanted to know Esther's nation, but she wouldn't tell him. He made a great feast for her so that she would be so happy that she would tell — but his plan didn't work. Then he tried to frighten her into telling, by saying he was gathering beautiful girls for a second time, to pick a new Queen. But she still wouldn't tell (*Megillah* 13a).

Finally Esther came to the King. He liked her so much that he made her his Queen.
The King was so happy that he made a big party.

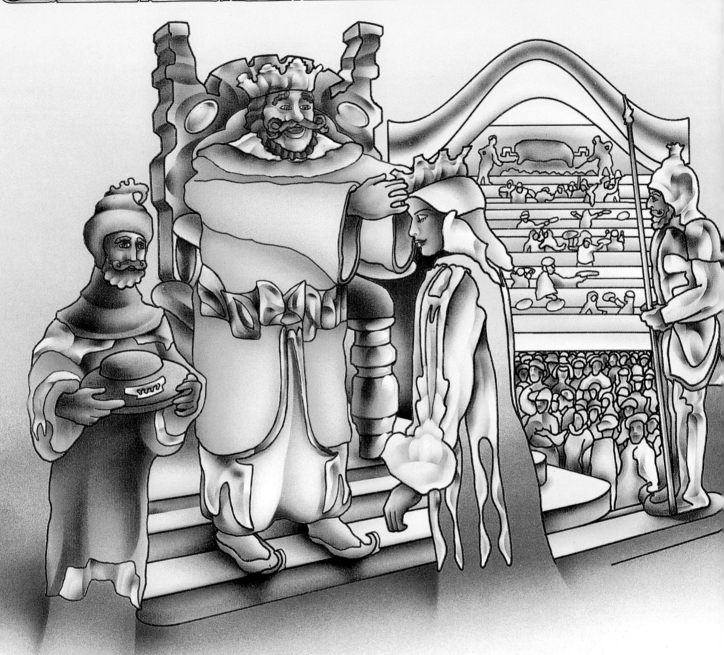

liked Esther more than all the women, and he favored and approved of her more than of all the other girls; so he put the royal crown on her head, and made her Queen in place of Vashti. ¹⁸Then the King made a great feast for all his officers and his servants — it was a feast in honor of Esther — and he said that the people in his countries would not have to pay taxes, and he gave out the kind of gifts that only a King can afford.

אֶת־אֶסְתֵּר מִכָּל־הַנָּשִׁים וַתִּשָּׂא־חֵן וָחֶסֶד לְפָנָיו מִכָּל־הַבְּתוּלֹת וַיָּשֶׂם כֶּתֶר־מַלְכוּת בְּרֹאשָׁהּ וַיַּמְלִיכֶהָ תַּחַת וַשְׁתִּי: יח וַיַּעַשׂ הַמֶּלֶךְ מִשְׁתֶּה גָדוֹל לְכָל־שָׂרָיו וַעֲבָדָיו אֵת מִשְׁתֵּה אֶסְתֵּר וַהֲנָחָה לַמְּדִינוֹת עָשָׂה וַיִּתֵּן מַשְׂאֵת כְּיַד הַמֶּלֶךְ:

One day, Mordechai heard two soldiers planning to kill the King. He told Esther. She told the King. They wrote in his record book that Mordechai had saved his life.

¹⁹The girls were brought together another time; and Mordechai used to sit at the King's gate. ²⁰Esther still did not tell where she was born or what nation she was from, as Mordechai had ordered her; for Esther still did as Mordechai said — just as she used to do when he was raising her.

In those days when Mordechai was sitting at the King's gate, Bigsan and Teresh were two of the King's servants who guarded the palace entrance. They became angry at King Achashveirosh and wanted to kill him. ²²Mordechai heard about the plot and told Queen Esther about it. Esther told the King about it and said that Mordechai had told her. ²³The story was investigated and found to be true. Bigsan and Teresh were hanged on a gallows, and the story was written in the King's private record book.

יט וּבְהִקָּבֵץ בְּתוּלוֹת שֵׁנִית וּמָרְדֳּכַי יֹשֵׁב בְּשַׁעַר־הַמֶּלֶךְ: כ אֵין אֶסְתֵּר מַגֶּדֶת מוֹלַדְתָּהּ וְאֶת־עַמָּהּ כַּאֲשֶׁר צִוָּה עָלֶיהָ מָרְדֳּכָי וְאֶת־מַאֲמַר מָרְדֳּכַי אֶסְתֵּר עֹשָׂה כַּאֲשֶׁר הָיְתָה בְאָמְנָה אִתּוֹ:

בַּיָּמִים הָהֵם וּמָרְדֳּכַי יוֹשֵׁב בְּשַׁעַר־הַמֶּלֶךְ קָצַף בִּגְתָן וָתֶרֶשׁ שְׁנֵי־סָרִיסֵי הַמֶּלֶךְ מִשֹּׁמְרֵי הַסַּף וַיְבַקְשׁוּ לִשְׁלֹחַ יָד בַּמֶּלֶךְ אֲחַשְׁוֵרֹשׁ: כב וַיִּוָּדַע הַדָּבָר לְמָרְדֳּכַי וַיַּגֵּד לְאֶסְתֵּר הַמַּלְכָּה וַתֹּאמֶר אֶסְתֵּר לַמֶּלֶךְ בְּשֵׁם מָרְדֳּכָי: כג וַיְבֻקַּשׁ הַדָּבָר וַיִּמָּצֵא וַיִּתָּלוּ שְׁנֵיהֶם עַל־עֵץ וַיִּכָּתֵב בְּסֵפֶר דִּבְרֵי הַיָּמִים לִפְנֵי הַמֶּלֶךְ:

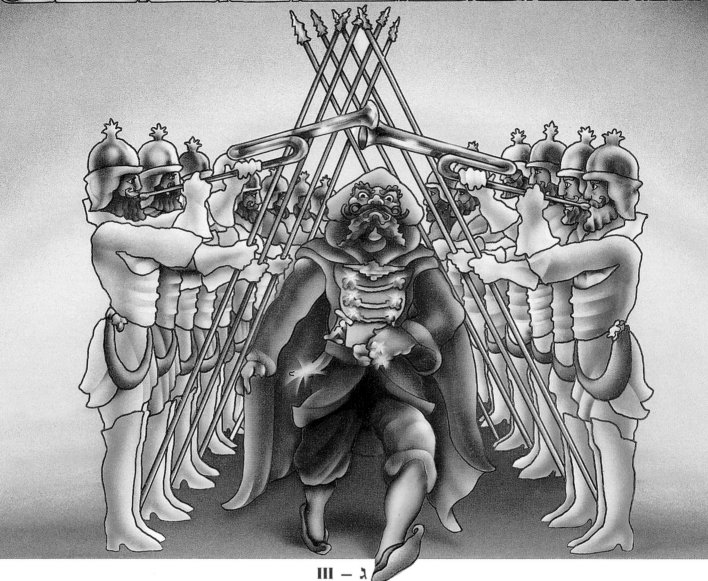

Achashveirosh had a wicked servant named Haman. The King made Haman
his chief officer and said that everyone must bow down to him.

III — ג

After these things happened, King Achash-veirosh promoted Haman, the son of Hamedasa the Agagite, and gave him a high rank; he made him more important than all the other royal officers. ²All the King's servants at the royal gate would have to get on their knees and bow before Haman, for this is what the King had ordered everyone to do for him. But Mordechai would not get on his knees and would not bow.

אַחַר ׀ הַדְּבָרִים הָאֵלֶּה גִּדַּל הַמֶּלֶךְ
אֲחַשְׁוֵרוֹשׁ אֶת־הָמָן בֶּן־הַמְּדָתָא
הָאֲגָגִי וַיְנַשְּׂאֵהוּ וַיָּשֶׂם אֶת־כִּסְאוֹ מֵעַל כָּל־
הַשָּׂרִים אֲשֶׁר אִתּוֹ: בּ וְכָל־עַבְדֵי הַמֶּלֶךְ אֲשֶׁר־
בְּשַׁעַר הַמֶּלֶךְ כֹּרְעִים וּמִשְׁתַּחֲוִים לְהָמָן כִּי־
כֵן צִוָּה־לוֹ הַמֶּלֶךְ וּמָרְדֳּכַי לֹא יִכְרַע וְלֹא
יִשְׁתַּחֲוֶה:

The Greater They Are the Harder They Fall. Some years earlier, the King had allowed the Jews in Jerusalem to begin building the *Beis Hamikdash*. However, Haman soon convinced the King to make them stop their building. At that time, Haman was an unimportant official. *Hashem* said, "If I punish him now, when he is not important, no one will know who he was. I will let him become famous. *Then* he will be hanged" (*Midrash*).

19 / YOUTH MEGILLAH

**Mordechai would not bow down to Haman.
Haman was so angry at Mordechai that he wanted to kill all the Jews.**

³So the King's servants at the King's gate asked Mordechai, "Why do you disobey the King's order?"

⁴When they said this to Mordechai day after day and he did not listen to them, they told Haman about him, to see if Mordechai would succeed — for he had told them that he was a Jew.

⁵When Haman saw that Mordechai would not bend his knee or bow before him, Haman was filled with anger. ⁶However he thought it would be a shame to punish only Mordechai, because they had told him that Mordechai was Jewish. So Haman wanted to destroy Mordechai's people — all the Jews in the entire kingdom of Achashveirosh.

גוַיֹּאמְרוּ עַבְדֵי הַמֶּלֶךְ אֲשֶׁר־בְּשַׁעַר הַמֶּלֶךְ
לְמָרְדֳּכָי מַדּוּעַ אַתָּה עוֹבֵר אֵת מִצְוַת הַמֶּלֶךְ:
דוַיְהִי °כְּאָמְרָם אֵלָיו יוֹם וָיוֹם וְלֹא שָׁמַע
אֲלֵיהֶם וַיַּגִּידוּ לְהָמָן לִרְאוֹת הֲיַעַמְדוּ דִּבְרֵי
מָרְדֳּכַי כִּי־הִגִּיד לָהֶם אֲשֶׁר־הוּא יְהוּדִי:
הוַיַּרְא הָמָן כִּי־אֵין מָרְדֳּכַי כֹּרֵעַ וּמִשְׁתַּחֲוֶה
לוֹ וַיִּמָּלֵא הָמָן חֵמָה: ווַיִּבֶז בְּעֵינָיו לִשְׁלֹחַ יָד
בְּמָרְדֳּכַי לְבַדּוֹ כִּי־הִגִּידוּ לוֹ אֶת־עַם מָרְדֳּכָי
וַיְבַקֵּשׁ הָמָן לְהַשְׁמִיד אֶת־כָּל־הַיְּהוּדִים אֲשֶׁר
בְּכָל־מַלְכוּת אֲחַשְׁוֵרוֹשׁ עַם מָרְדֳּכָי:

°בְּאָמְרָם כ'

Not Only Mordechai. Haman wanted an excuse to kill Mordechai, so he wore an idol on his clothes. He knew that Mordechai would never bow to an idol. Then he talked the King into making a law that everyone had to bow to *Haman.* Since Mordechai would not bow, he would be breaking the King's law and Haman would have him killed! But Haman knew that the reason Mordechai didn't bow was because the Torah says not to bow to an idol. So he decided to kill everyone who believed in the Torah (*Akeidas Yitzchak; Sefas Emes*).

Haman wanted to find a lucky day to kill the Jews. He made a lottery to pick a day. Then Haman went to talk Achashveirosh into letting him do it.

n the first month, the month of Nissan, in the twelfth year after Achashveirosh became King, they made a pur (that means a lottery) in front of Haman, to pick the best day, and the best month. The lottery picked the twelfth month of the year, which is the month of Adar.

בַּחֹדֶשׁ הָרִאשׁוֹן הוּא־חֹדֶשׁ נִיסָן בִּשְׁנַת שְׁתֵּים עֶשְׂרֵה לַמֶּלֶךְ אֲחַשְׁוֵרוֹשׁ הִפִּיל פּוּר הוּא הַגּוֹרָל לִפְנֵי הָמָן מִיּוֹם ׀ לְיוֹם וּמֵחֹדֶשׁ לְחֹדֶשׁ שְׁנֵים־עָשָׂר הוּא־חֹדֶשׁ אֲדָר:

⁸Then Haman told King Achashveirosh:

There is a certain nation scattered and spread out among the nations in all the countries of your kingdom. Their laws are different from the laws of every other nation. They do not even follow the King's laws; so it does not pay for the King to let them stay alive. ⁹If it pleases the King, let a law be written that they should be destroyed; and I will count out ten thousand silver talents to the King's workers to put into the royal treasuries.

ח וַיֹּאמֶר הָמָן לַמֶּלֶךְ אֲחַשְׁוֵרוֹשׁ יֶשְׁנוֹ עַם־אֶחָד מְפֻזָּר וּמְפֹרָד בֵּין הָעַמִּים בְּכֹל מְדִינוֹת מַלְכוּתֶךָ וְדָתֵיהֶם שֹׁנוֹת מִכָּל־עָם וְאֶת־דָּתֵי הַמֶּלֶךְ אֵינָם עֹשִׂים וְלַמֶּלֶךְ אֵין־שֹׁוֶה לְהַנִּיחָם: ט אִם־עַל־הַמֶּלֶךְ טוֹב יִכָּתֵב לְאַבְּדָם וַעֲשֶׂרֶת אֲלָפִים כִּכַּר־כֶּסֶף אֶשְׁקוֹל עַל־יְדֵי עֹשֵׂי הַמְּלָאכָה לְהָבִיא אֶל־גִּנְזֵי הַמֶּלֶךְ:

Fair Trade. Haman and Achashveirosh *both* hated the Jews. When Haman said he wanted to kill them, it was just what the King wanted to hear. He didn't even want Haman's money. These two enemies of the Jews were like two farmers. One had a hill of sand in his field and the other had a hole. The one with the hole said, ''I will give you a lot of

money for your sand. I need it to fill my hole.''

The other man said, ''I don't want your money. You will be doing me a big favor if you take away my sand!''

In the same way, Achashveirosh told Haman, ''I don't want your money. I will be very thankful if you get rid of the Jews for me'' (*Megillah* 14a).

¹⁰So the King took off his ring that had the royal seal on it, and gave it to Haman, the son of Hamedasa the Agagite, the enemy of the Jews. ¹¹And the King said to Haman, "Keep the silver, and do whatever you want with the nation."

י וַיָּ֨סַר הַמֶּ֜לֶךְ אֶת־טַבַּעְתּ֗וֹ מֵעַ֣ל יָד֔וֹ וַיִּתְּנָ֖הּ לְהָמָ֛ן בֶּֽן־הַמְּדָ֥תָא הָאֲגָגִ֖י צֹרֵ֥ר הַיְּהוּדִֽים: יא וַיֹּ֤אמֶר הַמֶּ֙לֶךְ֙ לְהָמָ֔ן הַכֶּ֖סֶף נָת֣וּן לָ֑ךְ וְהָעָ֕ם לַעֲשׂ֥וֹת בּ֖וֹ כַּטּ֥וֹב בְּעֵינֶֽיךָ:

¹²The King's secretaries were called on the thirteenth day of Nissan, and they wrote everything exactly as Haman ordered them. It was addressed to the King's rulers, to the governors of every country, and to the officers of every nation; to each country in its own script and each nation in its own language. It was written in King Achashveirosh's name, and it was sealed with the King's ring. ¹³Swift messengers delivered letters to all the King's countries, telling people to destroy, to kill, and to wipe out all the Jews, young and old, children and women, on the same day, the thirteenth day of the twelfth month, which is the month of Adar, and to steal their property.

יב וַיִּקָּרְא֣וּ סֹפְרֵ֨י הַמֶּ֜לֶךְ בַּחֹ֣דֶשׁ הָרִאשׁ֗וֹן בִּשְׁלוֹשָׁ֨ה עָשָׂ֣ר יוֹם֘ בּוֹ֒ וַיִּכָּתֵ֣ב כְּֽכָל־אֲשֶׁר־צִוָּ֣ה הָמָ֡ן אֶ֣ל אֲחַשְׁדַּרְפְּנֵֽי־הַמֶּ֣לֶךְ וְֽאֶל־הַפַּחוֹת֩ אֲשֶׁ֨ר ׀ עַל־מְדִינָ֜ה וּמְדִינָ֗ה וְאֶל־שָׂ֤רֵי עַם֙ וָעָ֔ם מְדִינָ֤ה וּמְדִינָה֙ כִּכְתָבָ֔הּ וְעַ֥ם וָעָ֖ם כִּלְשׁוֹנ֑וֹ בְּשֵׁ֨ם הַמֶּ֤לֶךְ אֲחַשְׁוֵרֹשׁ֙ נִכְתָּ֔ב וְנֶחְתָּ֖ם בְּטַבַּ֥עַת הַמֶּֽלֶךְ: יג וְנִשְׁל֨וֹחַ סְפָרִ֜ים בְּיַ֣ד הָרָצִים֮ אֶל־כָּל־מְדִינ֣וֹת הַמֶּלֶךְ֒ לְהַשְׁמִ֣יד לַהֲרֹ֣ג וּלְאַבֵּ֡ד אֶת־כָּל־הַ֠יְּהוּדִ֠ים מִנַּ֨עַר וְעַד־זָקֵ֜ן טַ֤ף וְנָשִׁים֙ בְּי֣וֹם אֶחָ֔ד בִּשְׁלוֹשָׁ֥ה עָשָׂ֛ר לְחֹ֥דֶשׁ שְׁנֵים־עָשָׂ֖ר הוּא־חֹ֣דֶשׁ אֲדָ֑ר וּשְׁלָלָ֖ם לָבֽוֹז:

[14]The contents of the letter were as follows: This law should be announced in every country for all the nations to know that they should be ready to fight on that day. [15]The swift messengers left in a great hurry as the King ordered them to do, and the law was announced in Shushan the Capital. Then the King and Haman sat down to drink, but the Jews of Shushan were confused.

יד פַּתְשֶׁגֶן הַכְּתָב לְהִנָּתֵן דָּת בְּכָל־מְדִינָה וּמְדִינָה גָּלוּי לְכָל־הָעַמִּים לִהְיוֹת עֲתִדִים לַיּוֹם הַזֶּה: טו הָרָצִים יָצְאוּ דְחוּפִים בִּדְבַר הַמֶּלֶךְ וְהַדָּת נִתְּנָה בְּשׁוּשַׁן הַבִּירָה וְהַמֶּלֶךְ וְהָמָן יָשְׁבוּ לִשְׁתּוֹת וְהָעִיר שׁוּשָׁן נָבוֹכָה:

Confusion in Shushan. The Jews could not understand why the Persians did not act the way they used to. If a Jew went to the store to buy food for his family, the Persian storekeeper would tease him and embarrass him by saying, "Soon I will kill you and take away everything you own!" (*Midrash*).

When Mordechai heard about the law, he put on clothes made of rough cloth to show
how sad he was. Then he went to Esther's palace.

ד – IV

Mordechai learned of all that had happened; and Mordechai tore his clothes and put on sackcloth and ashes. He went out into the middle of the city, and cried loudly and bitterly. ²He stopped in front of the King's gate for no one was allowed to enter the King's gate wearing sackcloth. ³Meanwhile, in every country, as far as the King's word and and his law went, there was great sadness among the Jews, with fasting, and weeping, and loud crying; most of the Jews sat on the ground, on sackcloth and ashes.

וּמָרְדֳּכַ֗י יָדַע֙ אֶת־כָּל־אֲשֶׁ֣ר נַעֲשָׂ֔ה וַיִּקְרַ֤ע מָרְדֳּכַי֙ אֶת־בְּגָדָ֔יו וַיִּלְבַּ֥שׁ שַׂ֖ק וָאֵ֑פֶר וַיֵּצֵא֙ בְּת֣וֹךְ הָעִ֔יר וַיִּזְעַ֛ק זְעָקָ֥ה גְדוֹלָ֖ה וּמָרָֽה: ב וַיָּב֕וֹא עַ֖ד לִפְנֵ֣י שַֽׁעַר־הַמֶּ֑לֶךְ כִּ֣י אֵ֥ין לָב֛וֹא אֶל־שַׁ֥עַר הַמֶּ֖לֶךְ בִּלְב֥וּשׁ שָֽׂק: ג וּבְכָל־מְדִינָ֣ה וּמְדִינָ֗ה מְקוֹם֙ אֲשֶׁ֨ר דְּבַר־הַמֶּ֤לֶךְ וְדָתוֹ֙ מַגִּ֔יעַ אֵ֤בֶל גָּדוֹל֙ לַיְּהוּדִ֔ים וְצ֥וֹם וּבְכִ֖י וּמִסְפֵּ֑ד שַׂ֣ק וָאֵ֔פֶר יֻצַּ֖ע לָֽרַבִּֽים:

⁴And Esther's maids and servants came and told her about it, and the Queen was very upset. She sent clothes for Mordechai to put on instead of his sackcloth, but he would not accept them.

⁵Then Esther called Hasach, one of the servants whom the King had appointed to serve her, and ordered him to go to Mordechai, to find out what was happening. ⁶So Hasach went out to Mordechai to the city square, which was in front of the King's gate. ⁷Mordechai told him everything that had happened to him, and all about the sum of money that Haman had promised to give to the royal treasury to pay for the murder of the Jews. ⁸Mordechai also gave Hasach a copy of the law that was given out in Shushan saying that the Jews should be destroyed. He wanted Hasach to show it to Esther and explain it to her — and then order her to go to the King, to beg him, and to plead with him for her people.

ד °וַתָּבוֹאנָה נַעֲרוֹת אֶסְתֵּר וְסָרִיסֶיהָ וַיַּגִּידוּ לָהּ וַתִּתְחַלְחַל הַמַּלְכָּה מְאֹד וַתִּשְׁלַח בְּגָדִים לְהַלְבִּישׁ אֶת־מָרְדֳּכַי וּלְהָסִיר שַׂקּוֹ מֵעָלָיו וְלֹא קִבֵּל:

ה וַתִּקְרָא אֶסְתֵּר לַהֲתָךְ מִסָּרִיסֵי הַמֶּלֶךְ אֲשֶׁר הֶעֱמִיד לְפָנֶיהָ וַתְּצַוֵּהוּ עַל־מָרְדֳּכָי לָדַעַת מַה־זֶּה וְעַל־מַה־זֶּה: וַיֵּצֵא הֲתָךְ אֶל־מָרְדֳּכָי אֶל־רְחוֹב הָעִיר אֲשֶׁר לִפְנֵי שַׁעַר־הַמֶּלֶךְ: ז וַיַּגֶּד־לוֹ מָרְדֳּכַי אֵת כָּל־אֲשֶׁר קָרָהוּ וְאֵת ׀ פָּרָשַׁת הַכֶּסֶף אֲשֶׁר אָמַר הָמָן לִשְׁקוֹל עַל־גִּנְזֵי הַמֶּלֶךְ °בַּיְּהוּדִים לְאַבְּדָם: ח וְאֶת־פַּתְשֶׁגֶן כְּתָב־הַדָּת אֲשֶׁר־נִתַּן בְּשׁוּשָׁן לְהַשְׁמִידָם נָתַן לוֹ לְהַרְאוֹת אֶת־אֶסְתֵּר וּלְהַגִּיד לָהּ וּלְצַוּוֹת עָלֶיהָ לָבוֹא אֶל־הַמֶּלֶךְ לְהִתְחַנֶּן־לוֹ וּלְבַקֵּשׁ מִלְּפָנָיו עַל־עַמָּהּ:

°וּתְבוֹאֶינָה כ' בַּיְּהוּדִיִּים כ'

Who Was Hasach? Hasach's real name was Daniel. He was a great *tzaddik* and he was once the most important Jew in the whole country. Esther sent him to Mordechai because she knew she could trust him to keep a secret (*Megillah* 15a).

⁹Hasach came and told Esther what Mordechai had said. ¹⁰Then Esther sent Hasach back to Mordechai with this message:

¹¹All the King's servants and the people of the King's countries know that if any man or woman comes to the King in his inner court without being called — no matter who it is, the law is the same — he is killed. But if the King points his gold scepter at that person, then that person will live. Now I have not been called to the King for the past thirty days.

¹²They told Esther's words to Mordechai.

¹³Then Mordechai said to answer Esther:

Do not think that you have a better chance than the rest of the Jews to escape in the King's palace. ¹⁴For if you stay quiet at a time like this, relief and rescue will come to the Jews from some other place, but you and your father's house will die. And who knows — maybe it was just for a time like this that you became Queen!

¹⁵And Esther said to answer Mordechai:

ט וַיָּבוֹא הֲתָךְ וַיַּגֵּד לְאֶסְתֵּר אֵת דִּבְרֵי מָרְדֳּכָי: י וַתֹּאמֶר אֶסְתֵּר לַהֲתָךְ וַתְּצַוֵּהוּ אֶל־מָרְדֳּכָי: יא כָּל־עַבְדֵי הַמֶּלֶךְ וְעַם מְדִינוֹת הַמֶּלֶךְ יֹדְעִים אֲשֶׁר כָּל־אִישׁ וְאִשָּׁה אֲשֶׁר־יָבוֹא אֶל־הַמֶּלֶךְ אֶל־הֶחָצֵר הַפְּנִימִית אֲשֶׁר לֹא־יִקָּרֵא אַחַת דָּתוֹ לְהָמִית לְבַד מֵאֲשֶׁר יוֹשִׁיט־לוֹ הַמֶּלֶךְ אֶת־שַׁרְבִיט הַזָּהָב וְחָיָה וַאֲנִי לֹא נִקְרֵאתִי לָבוֹא אֶל־הַמֶּלֶךְ זֶה שְׁלוֹשִׁים יוֹם: יב וַיַּגִּידוּ לְמָרְדֳּכָי אֵת דִּבְרֵי אֶסְתֵּר: יג וַיֹּאמֶר מָרְדֳּכַי לְהָשִׁיב אֶל־אֶסְתֵּר אַל־תְּדַמִּי בְנַפְשֵׁךְ לְהִמָּלֵט בֵּית־הַמֶּלֶךְ מִכָּל־הַיְּהוּדִים: יד כִּי אִם־הַחֲרֵשׁ תַּחֲרִישִׁי בָּעֵת הַזֹּאת רֶוַח וְהַצָּלָה יַעֲמוֹד לַיְּהוּדִים מִמָּקוֹם אַחֵר וְאַתְּ וּבֵית־אָבִיךְ תֹּאבֵדוּ וּמִי יוֹדֵעַ אִם־לְעֵת כָּזֹאת הִגַּעַתְּ לַמַּלְכוּת: טו וַתֹּאמֶר אֶסְתֵּר לְהָשִׁיב אֶל־מָרְדֳּכָי:

Let's Wait. Esther told Mordechai that she could be killed if she went to the King without permission. Even if the King would be kind enough to save her life, she would have to be so thankful that it would not be possible for her to ask him for such a big favor.

But Esther really wanted to help. She said, "Achashveirosh has not called me for thirty days. He will probably send for me in the next few days. Then, I will ask him" (*Malbim*).

Esther said she would risk her life to help her fellow Jews, but only if they fast and pray for her for three days. She and her maids would fast, too.

[16]Go, gather all the Jews who are in Shushan, and fast for me. Do not eat or drink for three days, night and day; I, with my maids, will fast also. Then I will go to the King, even though it is against the law. And if I die — then I will die.

[17]Then Mordechai left and did exactly what Esther had told him to do.

טז לֵךְ כְּנוֹס אֶת־כָּל־הַיְּהוּדִים הַנִּמְצְאִים בְּשׁוּשָׁן וְצוּמוּ עָלַי וְאַל־תֹּאכְלוּ וְאַל־תִּשְׁתּוּ שְׁלֹשֶׁת יָמִים לַיְלָה וָיוֹם גַּם־אֲנִי וְנַעֲרֹתַי אָצוּם כֵּן וּבְכֵן אָבוֹא אֶל־הַמֶּלֶךְ אֲשֶׁר לֹא־כַדָּת וְכַאֲשֶׁר אָבַדְתִּי אָבָדְתִּי: יז וַיַּעֲבֹר מָרְדֳּכָי וַיַּעַשׂ כְּכֹל אֲשֶׁר־צִוְּתָה עָלָיו אֶסְתֵּר:

Why Was Mordechai in a Hurry? Even though the thirteenth day of Adar, the day on which Haman would try to kill the Jews, was eleven months away, Mordechai didn't want to wait for even one day. "Right now," he said, "the Jews are ready to pray to *Hashem*. And it is the month of Nissan, the month when *Hashem* has always helped us. If we wait too long, the people may lose hope and stop praying" (*Midrash*).

Three days later, Esther came to the King. He was happy to see her, so he pointed his scepter toward her. That meant that the soldiers were not allowed to kill her.

V – ה

 hree days later, Esther dressed herself in royal clothes and stood in the inner court of the King's palace. She faced the King's room while the King was sitting on his throne in his royal room, and he was facing the entrance where Esther stood. ²When the King saw Queen Esther standing in the court, he was pleased with her. The King pointed toward Esther the gold scepter that was in his hand, and Esther came near and touched the tip of the scepter.

וַיְהִי l בַּיּוֹם הַשְּׁלִישִׁי וַתִּלְבַּשׁ אֶסְתֵּר מַלְכוּת וַתַּעֲמֹד בַּחֲצַר בֵּית־הַמֶּלֶךְ הַפְּנִימִית נֹכַח בֵּית הַמֶּלֶךְ וְהַמֶּלֶךְ יוֹשֵׁב עַל־כִּסֵּא מַלְכוּתוֹ בְּבֵית הַמַּלְכוּת נֹכַח פֶּתַח הַבָּיִת: ב וַיְהִי כִרְאוֹת הַמֶּלֶךְ אֶת־אֶסְתֵּר הַמַּלְכָּה עֹמֶדֶת בֶּחָצֵר נָשְׂאָה חֵן בְּעֵינָיו וַיּוֹשֶׁט הַמֶּלֶךְ לְאֶסְתֵּר אֶת־שַׁרְבִיט הַזָּהָב אֲשֶׁר בְּיָדוֹ וַתִּקְרַב אֶסְתֵּר וַתִּגַּע בְּרֹאשׁ הַשַּׁרְבִיט:

Hashem Helps. When Achashveirosh saw Esther standing there without permission, he was so angry that he wanted her killed. Then *Hashem* did a hidden miracle. He made the King like her more than ever. Achashveirosh pointed his scepter toward her, to protect her from the soldiers. He said, "Esther, my Queen. Don't be afraid. This law is not meant for you. You may come to me any time you want to" (*Midrash*).

מגילת אסתר / 30

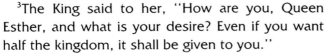

³The King said to her, "How are you, Queen Esther, and what is your desire? Even if you want half the kingdom, it shall be given to you."

⁴Esther said, "If it pleases the King, I would like the King and Haman to come today to the party that I have prepared for him."

⁵Then the King ordered, "Tell Haman to hurry and do as Esther said."

So the King and Haman came to the party that Esther had prepared.

⁶The King said to Esther during the wine party, "What is your request? It shall be given to you. And what is your desire? Even if it is half the kingdom, it shall be done."

⁷Esther answered and said:

This is my request and this is my desire: ⁸If the King is pleased with me, and if the King wishes to grant my request and do what I desire — let the King and Haman come to the party that I will prepare for them, and tomorrow I will tell the King what he wants to know.

ג וַיֹּאמֶר לָהּ הַמֶּלֶךְ מַה־לָּךְ אֶסְתֵּר הַמַּלְכָּה וּמַה־בַּקָּשָׁתֵךְ עַד־חֲצִי הַמַּלְכוּת וְיִנָּתֵן לָךְ: ד וַתֹּאמֶר אֶסְתֵּר אִם־עַל־הַמֶּלֶךְ טוֹב יָבוֹא הַמֶּלֶךְ וְהָמָן הַיּוֹם אֶל־הַמִּשְׁתֶּה אֲשֶׁר־עָשִׂיתִי לוֹ: ה וַיֹּאמֶר הַמֶּלֶךְ מַהֲרוּ אֶת־הָמָן לַעֲשׂוֹת אֶת־דְּבַר אֶסְתֵּר וַיָּבֹא הַמֶּלֶךְ וְהָמָן אֶל־הַמִּשְׁתֶּה אֲשֶׁר־עָשְׂתָה אֶסְתֵּר: ו וַיֹּאמֶר הַמֶּלֶךְ לְאֶסְתֵּר בְּמִשְׁתֵּה הַיַּיִן מַה־שְּׁאֵלָתֵךְ וְיִנָּתֵן לָךְ וּמַה־בַּקָּשָׁתֵךְ עַד־חֲצִי הַמַּלְכוּת וְתֵעָשׂ: ז וַתַּעַן אֶסְתֵּר וַתֹּאמַר שְׁאֵלָתִי וּבַקָּשָׁתִי: ח אִם־מָצָאתִי חֵן בְּעֵינֵי הַמֶּלֶךְ וְאִם־עַל־הַמֶּלֶךְ טוֹב לָתֵת אֶת־שְׁאֵלָתִי וְלַעֲשׂוֹת אֶת־בַּקָּשָׁתִי יָבוֹא הַמֶּלֶךְ וְהָמָן אֶל־הַמִּשְׁתֶּה אֲשֶׁר אֶעֱשֶׂה לָהֶם וּמָחָר אֶעֱשֶׂה כִּדְבַר הַמֶּלֶךְ:

hat day Haman went out happy and cheerful. But when Haman saw Mordechai in the King's gate, and Mordechai did not stand up or even move to show him respect, Haman became very angry with Mordechai. [10]But Haman controlled himself and went home. He sent for his friends and his wife, Zeresh. [11]Haman told them how proud he was of his wealth and of his many children and all about the times when the King had given him a high position and made him more important than the other officers and servants of the King.

[12]Haman said:

Not only that, but Queen Esther brought no one except me to be with the King at the party that she prepared. And for tomorrow also, I am invited to come to her with the King. [13]Yet all this means nothing to me as long as I see that Jew Mordechai sitting at the King's gate.

[14]Then his wife, Zeresh, and all his friends said to him:

Let us make a gallows fifty cubits high; and tomorrow morning you should get permission from the King to hang Mordechai on it. Then, you can be in a happy mood when you go with the King to the party.

Haman thought this was a good idea, and he made the gallows.

וַיֵּצֵא הָמָן בַּיּוֹם הַהוּא שָׂמֵחַ וְטוֹב לֵב וְכִרְאוֹת הָמָן אֶת־מָרְדֳּכַי בְּשַׁעַר הַמֶּלֶךְ וְלֹא־קָם וְלֹא־זָע מִמֶּנּוּ וַיִּמָּלֵא הָמָן עַל־מָרְדֳּכַי חֵמָה: י וַיִּתְאַפַּק הָמָן וַיָּבוֹא אֶל־בֵּיתוֹ וַיִּשְׁלַח וַיָּבֵא אֶת־אֹהֲבָיו וְאֶת־זֶרֶשׁ אִשְׁתּוֹ: יא וַיְסַפֵּר לָהֶם הָמָן אֶת־כְּבוֹד עָשְׁרוֹ וְרֹב בָּנָיו וְאֵת כָּל־אֲשֶׁר גִּדְּלוֹ הַמֶּלֶךְ וְאֵת אֲשֶׁר נִשְּׂאוֹ עַל־הַשָּׂרִים וְעַבְדֵי הַמֶּלֶךְ: יב וַיֹּאמֶר הָמָן אַף לֹא־הֵבִיאָה אֶסְתֵּר הַמַּלְכָּה עִם־הַמֶּלֶךְ אֶל־הַמִּשְׁתֶּה אֲשֶׁר־עָשָׂתָה כִּי אִם־אוֹתִי וְגַם־לְמָחָר אֲנִי קָרוּא־לָהּ עִם־הַמֶּלֶךְ: יג וְכָל־זֶה אֵינֶנּוּ שֹׁוֶה לִי בְּכָל־עֵת אֲשֶׁר אֲנִי רֹאֶה אֶת־מָרְדֳּכַי הַיְּהוּדִי יוֹשֵׁב בְּשַׁעַר הַמֶּלֶךְ: יד וַתֹּאמֶר לוֹ זֶרֶשׁ אִשְׁתּוֹ וְכָל־אֹהֲבָיו יַעֲשׂוּ־עֵץ גָּבֹהַּ חֲמִשִּׁים אַמָּה וּבַבֹּקֶר אֱמֹר לַמֶּלֶךְ וְיִתְלוּ אֶת־מָרְדֳּכַי עָלָיו וּבֹא עִם־הַמֶּלֶךְ אֶל־הַמִּשְׁתֶּה שָׂמֵחַ וַיִּיטַב הַדָּבָר לִפְנֵי הָמָן וַיַּעַשׂ הָעֵץ:

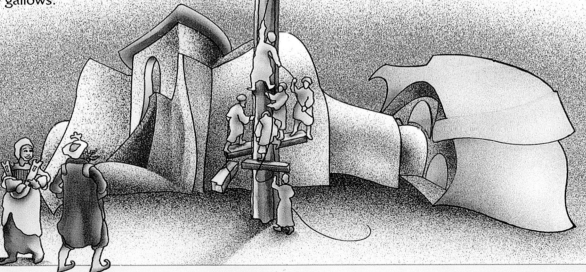

Haman's Gallows. Haman wanted his gallows to be so high that he would be able to see it even from the royal palace. Then he could see Mordechai hanging from it while he was drinking with Achashveirosh and Esther. Haman didn't even go to sleep that night. He and his sons helped the carpenters build the gallows. While they were working, Zeresh played music and when it was finished, she made a feast for everyone (Targum).

VI – ו

That night the King could not sleep well, so he ordered that they should bring his diary — his private history book — and that stories from it should be read to the King. ²It was found to be written that Mordechai had told about Bigsan and Teresh, two of the King's servants who guarded the palace entrance, who tried to kill King Achashveirosh.

³"What honor or reward has been given to Mordechai for this?" asked the King.

"Nothing has been done for him!" replied the King's servants.

⁴Then the King said, "Who is in the court?" (Haman had just come into the outer court of the palace to speak to the King about hanging Mordechai on the gallows that he had prepared for him.)

⁵So the King's servants answered him, "It is Haman standing in the court."

The King said, "Let him enter."

⁶When Haman came in, the King said to him, "What should be done for the man to whom the King wants to give a special honor?"

בַּלַּיְלָה הַהוּא נָדְדָה שְׁנַת הַמֶּלֶךְ וַיֹּאמֶר לְהָבִיא אֶת־סֵפֶר הַזִּכְרֹנוֹת דִּבְרֵי הַיָּמִים וַיִּהְיוּ נִקְרָאִים לִפְנֵי הַמֶּלֶךְ: ב וַיִּמָּצֵא כָתוּב אֲשֶׁר הִגִּיד מָרְדֳּכַי עַל־בִּגְתָנָא וָתֶרֶשׁ שְׁנֵי סָרִיסֵי הַמֶּלֶךְ מִשֹּׁמְרֵי הַסַּף אֲשֶׁר בִּקְשׁוּ לִשְׁלֹחַ יָד בַּמֶּלֶךְ אֲחַשְׁוֵרוֹשׁ:

ג וַיֹּאמֶר הַמֶּלֶךְ מַה־נַּעֲשָׂה יְקָר וּגְדוּלָּה לְמָרְדֳּכַי עַל־זֶה וַיֹּאמְרוּ נַעֲרֵי הַמֶּלֶךְ מְשָׁרְתָיו לֹא־נַעֲשָׂה עִמּוֹ דָּבָר:

ד וַיֹּאמֶר הַמֶּלֶךְ מִי בֶחָצֵר וְהָמָן בָּא לַחֲצַר בֵּית־הַמֶּלֶךְ הַחִיצוֹנָה לֵאמֹר לַמֶּלֶךְ לִתְלוֹת אֶת־מָרְדֳּכַי עַל־הָעֵץ אֲשֶׁר־הֵכִין לוֹ:

ה וַיֹּאמְרוּ נַעֲרֵי הַמֶּלֶךְ אֵלָיו הִנֵּה הָמָן עֹמֵד בֶּחָצֵר וַיֹּאמֶר הַמֶּלֶךְ יָבוֹא:

ו וַיָּבוֹא הָמָן וַיֹּאמֶר לוֹ הַמֶּלֶךְ מַה־לַּעֲשׂוֹת בָּאִישׁ אֲשֶׁר הַמֶּלֶךְ חָפֵץ בִּיקָרוֹ וַיֹּאמֶר הָמָן

The King's Sleep.

Achashveirosh kept waking up. He had a bad dream that Haman was trying to kill him with a sword (*Midrash*). Then the King began worrying that maybe Esther and Haman were making plans against him. He said to himself, "Why don't my friends warn me about people who want to hurt me?

Maybe someone once did me a big favor and I didn't reward him. Maybe that is why no one wants to help me." So Achashveirosh called a servant to read to him from his private record book. If the book showed that someone deserved a reward, Achashveirosh would give it to him right away (*Megillah* 15b).

Now Haman thought to himself, "Whom could the King want to honor more than me?"

[7] So Haman said to the King:

This is what should be done for the man whom the King wants to honor. [8] Have them bring a royal robe that the King himself has worn, and a horse that the King himself has ridden, and have a royal crown put on his head. [9] The robe and horse should be given to one of the King's highest officers. He should dress the man whom the King wants to honor, and lead him on horseback through the city square; and he should call out before him, "This is what is done for the man whom the King wants to honor."

[10] Then the King said to Haman, "Hurry, take the robe and the horse as you have said, and do all this for Mordechai the Jew, who sits at the King's gate. Do not leave out a single thing that you spoke about!"

[11] So Haman took the robe and the horse; he dressed Mordechai, and led him through the city square calling out before him, "This is what is done for the man whom the King wants to honor!"

ordechai went back to the King's gate; but Haman hurried home, sadly and with his head covered in shame. [13] Haman told his wife Zeresh and all his friends everything that had happened to him.

His advisors and his wife Zeresh said to him, "If Mordechai is Jewish — and you have started to lose to him — you will not be able to win against him, but you will surely lose to him."

[14] While they were still talking with him, the King's servants arrived, and they made Haman hurry to the party that Esther had prepared.

בְּלִבּוֹ לְמִי יַחְפֹּץ הַמֶּלֶךְ לַעֲשׂוֹת יְקָר יוֹתֵר מִמֶּנִּי: ז וַיֹּאמֶר הָמָן אֶל־הַמֶּלֶךְ אִישׁ אֲשֶׁר הַמֶּלֶךְ חָפֵץ בִּיקָרוֹ: ח יָבִיאוּ לְבוּשׁ מַלְכוּת אֲשֶׁר לָבַשׁ־בּוֹ הַמֶּלֶךְ וְסוּס אֲשֶׁר רָכַב עָלָיו הַמֶּלֶךְ וַאֲשֶׁר נִתַּן כֶּתֶר מַלְכוּת בְּרֹאשׁוֹ: ט וְנָתוֹן הַלְּבוּשׁ וְהַסּוּס עַל־יַד־אִישׁ מִשָּׂרֵי הַמֶּלֶךְ הַפַּרְתְּמִים וְהִלְבִּשׁוּ אֶת־הָאִישׁ אֲשֶׁר הַמֶּלֶךְ חָפֵץ בִּיקָרוֹ וְהִרְכִּיבֻהוּ עַל־הַסּוּס בִּרְחוֹב הָעִיר וְקָרְאוּ לְפָנָיו כָּכָה יֵעָשֶׂה לָאִישׁ אֲשֶׁר הַמֶּלֶךְ חָפֵץ בִּיקָרוֹ: י וַיֹּאמֶר הַמֶּלֶךְ לְהָמָן מַהֵר קַח אֶת־הַלְּבוּשׁ וְאֶת־הַסּוּס כַּאֲשֶׁר דִּבַּרְתָּ וַעֲשֵׂה־כֵן לְמָרְדֳּכַי הַיְּהוּדִי הַיּוֹשֵׁב בְּשַׁעַר הַמֶּלֶךְ אַל־תַּפֵּל דָּבָר מִכֹּל אֲשֶׁר דִּבַּרְתָּ: יא וַיִּקַּח הָמָן אֶת־הַלְּבוּשׁ וְאֶת־הַסּוּס וַיַּלְבֵּשׁ אֶת־מָרְדֳּכָי וַיַּרְכִּיבֵהוּ בִּרְחוֹב הָעִיר וַיִּקְרָא לְפָנָיו כָּכָה יֵעָשֶׂה לָאִישׁ אֲשֶׁר הַמֶּלֶךְ חָפֵץ בִּיקָרוֹ:

יב וַיָּשָׁב מָרְדֳּכַי אֶל־שַׁעַר הַמֶּלֶךְ וְהָמָן נִדְחַף אֶל־בֵּיתוֹ אָבֵל וַחֲפוּי רֹאשׁ: יג וַיְסַפֵּר הָמָן לְזֶרֶשׁ אִשְׁתּוֹ וּלְכָל־אֹהֲבָיו אֵת כָּל־אֲשֶׁר קָרָהוּ וַיֹּאמְרוּ לוֹ חֲכָמָיו וְזֶרֶשׁ אִשְׁתּוֹ אִם מִזֶּרַע הַיְּהוּדִים מָרְדֳּכַי אֲשֶׁר הַחִלּוֹתָ לִנְפֹּל לְפָנָיו לֹא־תוּכַל לוֹ כִּי־נָפוֹל תִּפּוֹל לְפָנָיו: יד עוֹדָם מְדַבְּרִים עִמּוֹ וְסָרִיסֵי הַמֶּלֶךְ הִגִּיעוּ וַיַּבְהִלוּ לְהָבִיא אֶת־הָמָן אֶל־הַמִּשְׁתֶּה אֲשֶׁר־עָשְׂתָה אֶסְתֵּר:

Which Mordechai? When Achashveirosh gave the order to honor Mordechai, poor Haman was shocked. "Who is Mordechai?" he asked.

Achashveirosh answered, "Mordechai the Jew!"

"But there must be many Jews named Mordechai!"

Achashveirosh added, "The one who sits at the palace gate!" (Megillah 16a).

Haman's Daughter. When Haman's daughter saw someone on a horse, being led by a man speaking of the King's honor, she was sure her father was on the horse and Mordechai was leading him. She took a pot of filthy garbage and dumped it on the head of the man leading the horse. When Haman looked up, his daughter saw what she had done to her own father. Then she jumped off the roof and died (Megillah 16a).

VII — ז

¹So the King and Haman came to drink with Queen Esther. ²The King asked Esther again on the second day at the wine party, "What is your request, Queen Esther? It will be given to you. And what is your desire? Even if it is half the kingdom, it shall be done."

³So Queen Esther answered and said:

If you are pleased with me, O King, and if the King wishes, I request that my own life be saved and I desire that the life of my nation be saved. ⁴For I and my nation have been sold to be destroyed, to be killed, and to be wiped out. Had we been sold as slaves and maidservants, I would have kept quiet, but our enemy does not care how much damage he causes the King.

א וַיָּבֹא הַמֶּלֶךְ וְהָמָן לִשְׁתּוֹת עִם־אֶסְתֵּר הַמַּלְכָּה: ב וַיֹּאמֶר הַמֶּלֶךְ לְאֶסְתֵּר גַּם בַּיּוֹם הַשֵּׁנִי בְּמִשְׁתֵּה הַיַּיִן מַה־שְּׁאֵלָתֵךְ אֶסְתֵּר הַמַּלְכָּה וְתִנָּתֵן לָךְ וּמַה־בַּקָּשָׁתֵךְ עַד־חֲצִי הַמַּלְכוּת וְתֵעָשׂ: ג וַתַּעַן אֶסְתֵּר הַמַּלְכָּה וַתֹּאמַר אִם־מָצָאתִי חֵן בְּעֵינֶיךָ הַמֶּלֶךְ וְאִם־עַל־הַמֶּלֶךְ טוֹב תִּנָּתֶן־לִי נַפְשִׁי בִּשְׁאֵלָתִי וְעַמִּי בְּבַקָּשָׁתִי: ד כִּי נִמְכַּרְנוּ אֲנִי וְעַמִּי לְהַשְׁמִיד לַהֲרוֹג וּלְאַבֵּד וְאִלּוּ לַעֲבָדִים וְלִשְׁפָחוֹת נִמְכַּרְנוּ הֶחֱרַשְׁתִּי כִּי אֵין הַצָּר שֹׁוֶה בְּנֵזֶק הַמֶּלֶךְ:

Two Kings. Esther said the word "King" twice in the same sentence. She was talking to two Kings at the same time. Not only was she speaking to Achashveirosh, she was also begging for the help of *Hashem*, the *real* King of the whole world (*Targum*).

Better to be Sold. Esther wanted to show Achashveirosh that Haman was not really his friend. She said, "If Haman truly loved you, he would have wanted you to sell the Jews as slaves. That way you would get money for them. It does not help you to let them be killed for nothing!" (*Rashi*).

⁵Then King Achashveirosh spoke up and said to Queen Esther, "Who is he? Where is the one who dared to do this?"

⁶Esther said, "An enemy and a foe! This wicked Haman!"

Haman trembled in fear before the King and Queen.

⁷The King stood up in anger. He left the wine party and went out to the palace garden, while Haman stayed there to beg Queen Esther for his life, because he saw that the King made up his mind to kill him.

⁸When the King came back from the palace garden to the room where the party was, Haman was kneeling on Esther's couch. The King said, "He even dares to attack the Queen while I am in the house!"

As soon as the King said this, the servants covered Haman's face. ⁹Then Charvonah, one of the officers who served the King, said, "Not only that, but there is a gallows that Haman made on which to hang Mordechai, the man who spoke up to help the King. The gallows is standing near Haman's house and it is fifty cubits high."

The King said, "Hang him on it!"

¹⁰So they hanged Haman on the gallows that he had prepared for Mordechai, and the King's anger calmed down.

ה וַיֹּאמֶר הַמֶּלֶךְ אֲחַשְׁוֵרוֹשׁ וַיֹּאמֶר לְאֶסְתֵּר הַמַּלְכָּה מִי הוּא זֶה וְאֵי־זֶה הוּא אֲשֶׁר־מְלָאוֹ לִבּוֹ לַעֲשׂוֹת כֵּן:

ו וַתֹּאמֶר אֶסְתֵּר אִישׁ צַר וְאוֹיֵב הָמָן הָרָע הַזֶּה וְהָמָן נִבְעַת מִלִּפְנֵי הַמֶּלֶךְ וְהַמַּלְכָּה:

ז וְהַמֶּלֶךְ קָם בַּחֲמָתוֹ מִמִּשְׁתֵּה הַיַּיִן אֶל־גִּנַּת הַבִּיתָן וְהָמָן עָמַד לְבַקֵּשׁ עַל־נַפְשׁוֹ מֵאֶסְתֵּר הַמַּלְכָּה כִּי רָאָה כִּי־כָלְתָה אֵלָיו הָרָעָה מֵאֵת הַמֶּלֶךְ:

ח וְהַמֶּלֶךְ שָׁב מִגִּנַּת הַבִּיתָן אֶל־בֵּית מִשְׁתֵּה הַיַּיִן וְהָמָן נֹפֵל עַל־הַמִּטָּה אֲשֶׁר אֶסְתֵּר עָלֶיהָ וַיֹּאמֶר הַמֶּלֶךְ הֲגַם לִכְבּוֹשׁ אֶת־הַמַּלְכָּה עִמִּי בַּבָּיִת הַדָּבָר יָצָא מִפִּי הַמֶּלֶךְ וּפְנֵי הָמָן חָפוּ: ט וַיֹּאמֶר חַרְבוֹנָה אֶחָד מִן־הַסָּרִיסִים לִפְנֵי הַמֶּלֶךְ גַּם הִנֵּה־הָעֵץ אֲשֶׁר־עָשָׂה הָמָן לְמָרְדֳּכַי אֲשֶׁר דִּבֶּר־טוֹב עַל־הַמֶּלֶךְ עֹמֵד בְּבֵית הָמָן גָּבֹהַּ חֲמִשִּׁים אַמָּה וַיֹּאמֶר הַמֶּלֶךְ תְּלֻהוּ עָלָיו:

י וַיִּתְלוּ אֶת־הָמָן עַל־הָעֵץ אֲשֶׁר־הֵכִין לְמָרְדֳּכָי וַחֲמַת הַמֶּלֶךְ שָׁכָכָה:

VIII – ח

That same day, King Achashveirosh gave the property of Haman, the enemy of the Jews, to Queen Esther, and Mordechai was invited to come to the King, for Esther had told him how they were related. ²The King took off his ring with the royal seal on it. He had taken it away from Haman, and now gave it to Mordechai. Then Esther put Mordechai in charge of Haman's property.

³Again, Esther spoke to the King. She fell down at his feet and cried. She begged him to stop the evil of Haman the Agagite, and the plan that he had

בַּיּוֹם הַהוּא נָתַן הַמֶּלֶךְ אֲחַשְׁוֵרוֹשׁ לְאֶסְתֵּר הַמַּלְכָּה אֶת־בֵּית הָמָן צֹרֵר הַיְּהוּדִים וּמָרְדֳּכַי בָּא לִפְנֵי הַמֶּלֶךְ כִּי־הִגִּידָה אֶסְתֵּר מָה הוּא־לָהּ: ב וַיָּסַר הַמֶּלֶךְ אֶת־טַבַּעְתּוֹ אֲשֶׁר הֶעֱבִיר מֵהָמָן וַיִּתְּנָהּ לְמָרְדֳּכָי וַתָּשֶׂם אֶסְתֵּר אֶת־מָרְדֳּכַי עַל־בֵּית הָמָן:

ג וַתּוֹסֶף אֶסְתֵּר וַתְּדַבֵּר לִפְנֵי הַמֶּלֶךְ וַתִּפֹּל לִפְנֵי רַגְלָיו וַתֵּבְךְּ וַתִּתְחַנֶּן־לוֹ לְהַעֲבִיר אֶת־רָעַת הָמָן הָאֲגָגִי וְאֵת מַחֲשַׁבְתּוֹ אֲשֶׁר חָשַׁב

°הַיְּהוּדִיִּים כ׳

Charvonah Speaks up. Charvonah was Haman's friend, and had wanted to help Haman hang Mordechai (*Megillah* 16a). He knew all about the plan to hang Mordechai, even how high the gallows was. But now that Charvonah saw that the King was so angry, he changed sides. He told Achashveirosh that Haman was so bad that he even built a gallows to hang the King's friend! If Charvonah had not done that, the King might not have said to kill Haman right away. And if Haman had been given more time to live, he was smart enough to figure out a way to save himself (*Yad Hamelech*).

Esther begged the King to take back the law that all the Jews should be killed. He said that the law could not be taken back, but Esther and Mordechai could add to it.

thought up against the Jews. [4]The King pointed the gold scepter toward Esther, and Esther got up and stood before the King.

[5]She said:

If the King wishes and if he is pleased with me, and if the King thinks that my idea is right, and if he thinks that I am good, let a law be written to bring back those letters that contained the plans of Haman the son of Hamedasa the Agagite, in which he wrote the order to destroy the Jews in all the King's countries. [6]For how can I bear to see the terrible thing that will happen to my nation! How can I bear to see the destruction of my family!

[7]Then King Achashveirosh said to Queen Esther and to Mordechai the Jew:

I have given Haman's property to Esther, and he has been hanged on the gallows because he plotted against the Jews. [8]You may write in the King's name whatever you want about the Jews, and seal it with the royal ring, but any law that was once written in the King's name and sealed with the royal ring may not be cancelled.

עַל־הַיְּהוּדִֽים: ד וַיּ֣וֹשֶׁט הַמֶּ֣לֶךְ לְאֶסְתֵּ֗ר אֵ֚ת שַׁרְבִ֣ט הַזָּהָ֔ב וַתָּ֥קׇם אֶסְתֵּ֖ר וַֽתַּעֲמֹ֥ד לִפְנֵ֥י הַמֶּֽלֶךְ:

ה וַ֠תֹּ֠אמֶר אִם־עַל־הַמֶּ֨לֶךְ ט֜וֹב וְאִם־מָצָ֧אתִי חֵ֣ן לְפָנָ֗יו וְכָשֵׁ֤ר הַדָּבָר֙ לִפְנֵ֣י הַמֶּ֔לֶךְ וְטוֹבָ֥ה אֲנִ֖י בְּעֵינָ֑יו יִכָּתֵ֞ב לְהָשִׁ֣יב אֶת־הַסְּפָרִ֗ים מַחֲשֶׁ֜בֶת הָמָ֤ן בֶּֽן־הַמְּדָ֙תָא֙ הָֽאֲגָגִ֔י אֲשֶׁ֣ר כָּתַ֗ב לְאַבֵּד֙ אֶת־הַיְּהוּדִ֔ים אֲשֶׁ֖ר בְּכׇל־מְדִינ֥וֹת הַמֶּֽלֶךְ: ו כִּ֠י אֵֽיכָכָ֤ה אוּכַל֙ וְֽרָאִ֔יתִי בָּרָעָ֖ה אֲשֶׁר־יִמְצָ֣א אֶת־עַמִּ֑י וְאֵֽיכָכָ֤ה אוּכַל֙ וְֽרָאִ֔יתִי בְּאׇבְדַ֖ן מֽוֹלַדְתִּֽי:

ז וַיֹּ֨אמֶר הַמֶּ֤לֶךְ אֲחַשְׁוֵרֹשׁ֙ לְאֶסְתֵּ֣ר הַמַּלְכָּ֔ה וּֽלְמׇרְדֳּכַ֖י הַיְּהוּדִ֑י הִנֵּ֨ה בֵית־הָמָ֜ן נָתַ֣תִּי לְאֶסְתֵּ֗ר וְאֹתוֹ֙ תָּל֣וּ עַל־הָעֵ֔ץ עַ֛ל אֲשֶׁר־שָׁלַ֥ח יָד֖וֹ בַּיְּהוּדִֽֿים°: ח וְ֠אַתֶּ֠ם כִּתְב֨וּ עַל־ הַיְּהוּדִ֜ים כַּטּ֤וֹב בְּעֵֽינֵיכֶם֙ בְּשֵׁ֣ם הַמֶּ֔לֶךְ וְחִתְמ֖וּ בְּטַבַּ֣עַת הַמֶּ֑לֶךְ כִּֽי־כְתָ֞ב אֲשֶׁר־נִכְתָּ֣ב בְּשֵׁם־ הַמֶּ֗לֶךְ וְנַחְתּ֛וֹם בְּטַבַּ֥עַת הַמֶּ֖לֶךְ אֵ֥ין לְהָשִֽׁיב:

°בַּיְּהוּדִיִּ֖ם כ'

מגילת אסתר / 38

Mordechai wrote a new law saying that the Jews were allowed to kill their enemies on the thirteenth of Adar. Fast riders delivered the law to all the countries.

⁹So the King's secretaries were called at that time, on the twenty-third day of the third month, which is the month of Sivan. The new law was written exactly as Mordechai said it should be. It was sent to the Jews and to the rulers, the governors, and officers of the countries from Hodu to Cush, a hundred and twenty-seven countries, to each country in its own script, to each nation in its own language, and to the Jews in their own script and language. ¹⁰He wrote the law in the name of the King Achashveirosh and sealed it with the King's ring. He sent out letters by swift messengers on horseback, and by riders of fast camels.

ט וַיִּקָּרְאוּ סֹפְרֵי־הַמֶּלֶךְ בָּעֵת־הַהִיא בַּחֹדֶשׁ הַשְּׁלִישִׁי הוּא־חֹדֶשׁ סִיוָן בִּשְׁלוֹשָׁה וְעֶשְׂרִים בּוֹ וַיִּכָּתֵב כְּכָל־אֲשֶׁר־צִוָּה מָרְדֳּכַי אֶל־הַיְּהוּדִים וְאֶל הָאֲחַשְׁדַּרְפְּנִים וְהַפַּחוֹת וְשָׂרֵי הַמְּדִינוֹת אֲשֶׁר | מֵהֹדּוּ וְעַד־כּוּשׁ שֶׁבַע וְעֶשְׂרִים וּמֵאָה מְדִינָה מְדִינָה וּמְדִינָה כִּכְתָבָהּ וְעַם וָעָם כִּלְשֹׁנוֹ וְאֶל־הַיְּהוּדִים כִּכְתָבָם וְכִלְשׁוֹנָם: י וַיִּכְתֹּב בְּשֵׁם הַמֶּלֶךְ אֲחַשְׁוֵרֹשׁ וַיַּחְתֹּם בְּטַבַּעַת הַמֶּלֶךְ וַיִּשְׁלַח סְפָרִים בְּיַד הָרָצִים בַּסּוּסִים רֹכְבֵי הָרֶכֶשׁ הָאֲחַשְׁתְּרָנִים בְּנֵי הָרַמָּכִים:

¹¹The letters said that the King had given permission to the Jews of every single city to join together and defend themselves: to destroy, to kill, and to wipe out the entire army — along with their wives and children — of any nation or country that wants to hurt them; and the Jews could take their enemies' property. ¹²All this should happen on the same day in all the countries of King Achashveirosh, on the thirteenth day of the twelfth month, which is the month of Adar. ¹³The contents of the letter were as follows: This law should be announced in every country for all the nations to know that on that day the Jews should be ready to take revenge against their enemies. ¹⁴The swift messengers, riders of fast camels, left in a very great hurry by order of the King, and the law was announced in Shushan the Capital.

יא אֲשֶׁר נָתַן הַמֶּלֶךְ לַיְּהוּדִים | אֲשֶׁר | בְּכָל־עִיר וָעִיר לְהִקָּהֵל וְלַעֲמֹד עַל־נַפְשָׁם לְהַשְׁמִיד וְלַהֲרֹג וּלְאַבֵּד אֶת־כָּל־חֵיל עַם וּמְדִינָה הַצָּרִים אֹתָם טַף וְנָשִׁים וּשְׁלָלָם לָבוֹז: יב בְּיוֹם אֶחָד בְּכָל־מְדִינוֹת הַמֶּלֶךְ אֲחַשְׁוֵרוֹשׁ בִּשְׁלוֹשָׁה עָשָׂר לְחֹדֶשׁ שְׁנֵים־עָשָׂר הוּא־חֹדֶשׁ אֲדָר: יג פַּתְשֶׁגֶן הַכְּתָב לְהִנָּתֵן דָּת בְּכָל־מְדִינָה וּמְדִינָה גָּלוּי לְכָל־הָעַמִּים וְלִהְיוֹת °הַיְּהוּדִים עֲתִידִים לַיּוֹם הַזֶּה לְהִנָּקֵם מֵאֹיְבֵיהֶם: יד הָרָצִים רֹכְבֵי הָרֶכֶשׁ הָאֲחַשְׁתְּרָנִים יָצְאוּ מְבֹהָלִים וּדְחוּפִים בִּדְבַר הַמֶּלֶךְ וְהַדָּת נִתְּנָה בְּשׁוּשַׁן הַבִּירָה:

°הַיְּהוּדִיים עתודים כ'

Joining Together. No matter what the law said, the Jews could not succeed in fighting their enemies unless *Hashem* would help them. Otherwise, the Amalekite enemies and their friends would fight back and attack the Jewish people. That is why the Jews had to "join together." When we are united and pray together, *Hashem* helps us (*D'na Pashra*).

Achashveirosh dressed Mordechai like a King, and the Jews in Shushan were very happy. The Jews were respected, and they became the masters of their enemies.

Mordechai left the King wearing blue and white royal clothes with a big gold crown and robes of fine linen and of purple wool; then the city of Shushan was cheerful and glad. [16] The Jews had light and gladness, and joy and honor. [17] The same thing happened in every country and in every city, wherever the King's command and his law reached, that the Jews had gladness and joy, a feast and a holiday. And many from among the nations of the land made believe they were Jews, because they had become afraid of the Jews.

וּמָרְדֳּכַ֞י יָצָ֣א ׀ מִלִּפְנֵ֣י הַמֶּ֗לֶךְ בִּלְב֤וּשׁ מַלְכוּת֙ תְּכֵ֣לֶת וָח֔וּר וַעֲטֶ֤רֶת זָהָב֙ גְּדוֹלָ֔ה וְתַכְרִ֥יךְ בּ֖וּץ וְאַרְגָּמָ֑ן וְהָעִ֣יר שׁוּשָׁ֔ן צָֽהֲלָ֖ה וְשָׂמֵֽחָה: טז לַיְּהוּדִ֕ים הָֽיְתָ֥ה אוֹרָ֖ה וְשִׂמְחָ֑ה וְשָׂשֹׂ֖ן וִיקָֽר: יז וּבְכָל־מְדִינָ֣ה וּמְדִינָ֗ה וּבְכָל־עִ֣יר וָעִ֔יר מְקוֹם֙ אֲשֶׁ֣ר דְּבַר־הַמֶּ֤לֶךְ וְדָתוֹ֙ מַגִּ֔יעַ שִׂמְחָ֤ה וְשָׂשׂוֹן֙ לַיְּהוּדִ֔ים מִשְׁתֶּ֖ה וְי֣וֹם ט֑וֹב וְרַבִּ֞ים מֵֽעַמֵּ֤י הָאָ֨רֶץ֙ מִֽתְיַֽהֲדִ֔ים כִּֽי־נָפַ֥ל פַּֽחַד־הַיְּהוּדִ֖ים עֲלֵיהֶֽם:

ט – IX

And so, on the thirteenth day of the twelfth month, the month of Adar, when the King's order and law were about to be carried out — on the very day that the enemies of the Jews expected to become their masters — the opposite happened: The Jews became the masters of their enemies!

[2] The Jews joined together in their cities all over the countries of King Achashveirosh, to attack those who wanted to hurt them; and no one stood in their way, because all the people were afraid of them. [3] And all the officers of the countries and the rulers,

וּבִשְׁנֵים֩ עָשָׂ֨ר חֹ֜דֶשׁ הוּא־חֹ֣דֶשׁ אֲדָ֗ר בִּשְׁלוֹשָׁ֨ה עָשָׂ֥ר יוֹם֙ בּ֔וֹ אֲשֶׁ֨ר הִגִּ֧יעַ דְּבַר־הַמֶּ֛לֶךְ וְדָת֖וֹ לְהֵֽעָשׂ֑וֹת בַּיּ֗וֹם אֲשֶׁ֨ר שִׂבְּר֜וּ אֹֽיְבֵ֤י הַיְּהוּדִים֙ לִשְׁל֣וֹט בָּהֶ֔ם וְנַֽהֲפ֣וֹךְ ה֔וּא אֲשֶׁ֨ר יִשְׁלְט֧וּ הַיְּהוּדִ֛ים הֵ֖מָּה בְּשֹֽׂנְאֵיהֶֽם: ב נִקְהֲל֨וּ הַיְּהוּדִ֜ים בְּעָֽרֵיהֶ֗ם בְּכָל־מְדִינוֹת֙ הַמֶּ֣לֶךְ אֲחַשְׁוֵר֔וֹשׁ לִשְׁלֹ֣חַ יָ֔ד בִּמְבַקְשֵׁ֖י רָֽעָתָ֑ם וְאִישׁ֙ לֹא־עָמַ֣ד לִפְנֵיהֶ֔ם כִּֽי־נָפַ֥ל פַּחְדָּ֖ם עַל־כָּל־הָֽעַמִּֽים: ג וְכָל־שָׂרֵ֣י הַמְּדִינ֡וֹת

³And all the officers of the countries and the rulers, the governors and those who worked for the King respected the Jews, because they were afraid of Mordechai. ⁴For Mordechai was now the most important person in the royal palace. He became famous in all the countries, because that man Mordechai was becoming more and more important.

⁵And the Jews fought all their enemies with the sword, killing and wiping them out; they did whatever they wanted to with their enemies. ⁶In Shushan the Capital, the Jews killed and wiped out five hundred men, ⁷including:

Parshandasa and
Dalphon and
Aspasa ⁸and
Porasa and
Adalia and
Aridasa ⁹and
Parmashta and
Arisai and
Aridai and
Vayzasa ¹⁰the ten sons of Haman, son of Hamedasa, enemy of the Jews; but they did not take any property.

¹¹On that day the King was told how many were killed in Shushan the Capital. ¹²The King said to Queen Esther:

In Shushan the Capital the Jews have killed and wiped out five hundred men, as well as the ten sons of Haman; just think what they must have done in the rest of the King's countries! What is your request now? It shall be given to you. What else do you desire? It shall be done.

וְהָאֲחַשְׁדַּרְפְּנִים וְהַפַּחוֹת וְעֹשֵׂי הַמְּלָאכָה
אֲשֶׁר לַמֶּלֶךְ מְנַשְּׂאִים אֶת־הַיְּהוּדִים כִּי־נָפַל
פַּחַד־מָרְדֳּכַי עֲלֵיהֶם: ד כִּי־גָדוֹל מָרְדֳּכַי
בְּבֵית הַמֶּלֶךְ וְשָׁמְעוֹ הוֹלֵךְ בְּכָל־הַמְּדִינוֹת
כִּי־הָאִישׁ מָרְדֳּכַי הוֹלֵךְ וְגָדוֹל:
ה וַיַּכּוּ הַיְּהוּדִים בְּכָל־אֹיְבֵיהֶם מַכַּת־חֶרֶב
וְהֶרֶג וְאַבְדָן וַיַּעֲשׂוּ בְשֹׂנְאֵיהֶם כִּרְצוֹנָם:
ו וּבְשׁוּשַׁן הַבִּירָה הָרְגוּ הַיְּהוּדִים וְאַבֵּד
חֲמֵשׁ מֵאוֹת אִישׁ: וְאֵת |
פַּרְשַׁנְדָּתָא וְאֵת |
דַּלְפוֹן וְאֵת |
אַסְפָּתָא: וְאֵת |
פּוֹרָתָא וְאֵת |
אֲדַלְיָא וְאֵת |
אֲרִידָתָא: וְאֵת |
פַּרְמַשְׁתָּא וְאֵת |
אֲרִיסַי וְאֵת |
אֲרִידַי וְאֵת |
וַיְזָתָא: עֲשֶׂרֶת
בְּנֵי הָמָן בֶּן־
הַמְּדָתָא צֹרֵר
הַיְּהוּדִים הָרָגוּ
וּבַבִּזָּה לֹא
שָׁלְחוּ אֶת־יָדָם: יא בַּיּוֹם הַהוּא בָּא
מִסְפַּר הַהֲרוּגִים בְּשׁוּשַׁן
הַבִּירָה לִפְנֵי הַמֶּלֶךְ: יב וַיֹּאמֶר
הַמֶּלֶךְ לְאֶסְתֵּר הַמַּלְכָּה בְּשׁוּשַׁן הַבִּירָה הָרְגוּ
הַיְּהוּדִים וְאַבֵּד חֲמֵשׁ מֵאוֹת אִישׁ וְאֵת עֲשֶׂרֶת
בְּנֵי־הָמָן בִּשְׁאָר מְדִינוֹת הַמֶּלֶךְ מֶה עָשׂוּ וּמַה־
שְּׁאֵלָתֵךְ וְיִנָּתֵן לָךְ וּמַה־בַּקָּשָׁתֵךְ עוֹד וְתֵעָשׂ:

Mordechai's Fame. At first people thought that the King had promoted Mordechai partly because Mordechai had once saved his life and partly because Mordechai was Esther's relative. But as people got to know Mordechai better, they realized that Mordechai was a very great man.

A Long Line. The names of Haman's sons and the word עֲשֶׂרֶת, *ten*, are read in one breath because those ten wicked people all died at the same time. The letter ו of וַיְזָתָא, *Vayzasa*, is written long, like a pole, because all ten sons were hung on their father's gallows, one under the other (*Megillah* 16b).

Esther asked the King to let the Jews in Shushan kill their enemies for one more day. In every city, the Jews rested on the day after they fought. They sent food to friends.

¹³Esther answered, ''If the King wishes, please let the Jews who live in Shushan do the same thing tomorrow that they did today, and let Haman's ten sons be hanged on the gallows.''

¹⁴The King ordered that this be done. An order was given in Shushan, and they hanged Haman's ten sons. ¹⁵The Jews that were in Shushan joined together on the fourteenth day of the month of Adar, and killed three hundred men in Shushan; but they did not take any property.

¹⁶The rest of the Jews in all the King's countries joined together and defended themselves, and rested from their enemies, killing seventy-five thousand of their enemies — but they did not take any property.

¹⁷That happened on the thirteenth day of Adar; and they rested on the fourteenth day, making it a day of feasting and gladness. ¹⁸But the Jews who lived in Shushan joined together to fight on both the thirteenth and fourteenth, and they rested on the fifteenth, making it a day of feasting and gladness.

¹⁹That is why Jews who are spread out and live in towns without walls make the fourteenth day of Adar a time of gladness, feasting, a holiday, and sending food to their friends.

יג וַתֹּאמֶר אֶסְתֵּר אִם־עַל־הַמֶּלֶךְ טוֹב יִנָּתֵן גַּם־מָחָר לַיְּהוּדִים אֲשֶׁר בְּשׁוּשָׁן לַעֲשׂוֹת כְּדָת הַיּוֹם וְאֵת עֲשֶׂרֶת בְּנֵי־הָמָן יִתְלוּ עַל־הָעֵץ: יד וַיֹּאמֶר הַמֶּלֶךְ לְהֵעָשׂוֹת כֵּן וַתִּנָּתֵן דָּת בְּשׁוּשָׁן וְאֵת עֲשֶׂרֶת בְּנֵי־הָמָן תָּלוּ: טו וַיִּקָּהֲלוּ הַיְּהוּדִים אֲשֶׁר־בְּשׁוּשָׁן גַּם בְּיוֹם אַרְבָּעָה עָשָׂר לְחֹדֶשׁ אֲדָר וַיַּהַרְגוּ בְשׁוּשָׁן שְׁלֹשׁ מֵאוֹת אִישׁ וּבַבִּזָּה לֹא שָׁלְחוּ אֶת־יָדָם: טז וּשְׁאָר הַיְּהוּדִים אֲשֶׁר בִּמְדִינוֹת הַמֶּלֶךְ נִקְהֲלוּ | וְעָמֹד עַל־נַפְשָׁם וְנוֹחַ מֵאֹיְבֵיהֶם וְהָרֹג בְּשֹׂנְאֵיהֶם חֲמִשָּׁה וְשִׁבְעִים אָלֶף וּבַבִּזָּה לֹא שָׁלְחוּ אֶת־יָדָם: יז בְּיוֹם־שְׁלוֹשָׁה עָשָׂר לְחֹדֶשׁ אֲדָר וְנוֹחַ בְּאַרְבָּעָה עָשָׂר בּוֹ וְעָשֹׂה אֹתוֹ יוֹם מִשְׁתֶּה וְשִׂמְחָה: יח וְהַיְּהוּדִים אֲשֶׁר־בְּשׁוּשָׁן נִקְהֲלוּ בִּשְׁלוֹשָׁה עָשָׂר בּוֹ וּבְאַרְבָּעָה עָשָׂר בּוֹ וְנוֹחַ בַּחֲמִשָּׁה עָשָׂר בּוֹ וְעָשֹׂה אֹתוֹ יוֹם מִשְׁתֶּה וְשִׂמְחָה: יט עַל־כֵּן הַיְּהוּדִים הַפְּרָזִים הַיֹּשְׁבִים בְּעָרֵי הַפְּרָזוֹת עֹשִׂים אֵת יוֹם אַרְבָּעָה עָשָׂר לְחֹדֶשׁ אֲדָר שִׂמְחָה וּמִשְׁתֶּה וְיוֹם טוֹב וּמִשְׁלֹחַ מָנוֹת אִישׁ לְרֵעֵהוּ:

°הַיְּהוּדִיִּים כ' וְהַיְּהוּדִיִּים כ' הַפְּרוֹזִים כ'

Mordechai wrote down everything that happened and sent letters to all the Jews in all the countries of King Achashveirosh, near and far. [21]He told them to celebrate the fourteenth and fifteenth days of Adar every year. [22]Those were the days when the Jews rested from their enemies, and that was the month that had been changed for them from sorrow to gladness, and from sadness to a holiday. Therefore, they should celebrate them as days of feasting and gladness, and of sending food to their friends and gifts to the poor. [23]The Jews promised to celebrate every year just as they began to do then — just as Mordechai had written to them.

[24]For Haman, the son of Hamedasa the Agagite, enemy of all the Jews, had plotted to destroy the Jews and had made a pur (that means a lottery) to frighten and destroy them. [25]But when Queen Esther came before the King, he sent letters ordering that the evil plan, that Haman had thought up against the Jews, should come back on his own head; and they hanged him and his sons on the gallows.

[26]That is why they called these days "Purim," from the word "pur." Therefore, because of all that was written in this letter, and because of what they had gone through and what had happened to them, [27]the Jews agreed and promised that they, their children and everyone who would become Jewish would keep these two days without fail, just as Mordechai had written, and at the same time every single year. [28]So these days should be remembered and celebrated by every single generation, by every family, in every country, and in every city. And these days of Purim will never stop being celebrated by the Jews, and their memory will never leave their children.

וַיִּכְתֹּב מָרְדֳּכַי אֶת־הַדְּבָרִים הָאֵלֶּה וַיִּשְׁלַח סְפָרִים אֶל־כָּל־הַיְּהוּדִים אֲשֶׁר בְּכָל־מְדִינוֹת הַמֶּלֶךְ אֲחַשְׁוֵרוֹשׁ הַקְּרוֹבִים וְהָרְחוֹקִים: כא לְקַיֵּם עֲלֵיהֶם לִהְיוֹת עֹשִׂים אֵת יוֹם אַרְבָּעָה עָשָׂר לְחֹדֶשׁ אֲדָר וְאֵת יוֹם־חֲמִשָּׁה עָשָׂר בּוֹ בְּכָל־שָׁנָה וְשָׁנָה: כב כַּיָּמִים אֲשֶׁר־נָחוּ בָהֶם הַיְּהוּדִים מֵאֹיְבֵיהֶם וְהַחֹדֶשׁ אֲשֶׁר נֶהְפַּךְ לָהֶם מִיָּגוֹן לְשִׂמְחָה וּמֵאֵבֶל לְיוֹם טוֹב לַעֲשׂוֹת אוֹתָם יְמֵי מִשְׁתֶּה וְשִׂמְחָה וּמִשְׁלֹחַ מָנוֹת אִישׁ לְרֵעֵהוּ וּמַתָּנוֹת לָאֶבְיֹנִים: כג וְקִבֵּל הַיְּהוּדִים אֵת אֲשֶׁר־הֵחֵלּוּ לַעֲשׂוֹת וְאֵת אֲשֶׁר־כָּתַב מָרְדֳּכַי אֲלֵיהֶם:

כד כִּי הָמָן בֶּן־הַמְּדָתָא הָאֲגָגִי צֹרֵר כָּל־הַיְּהוּדִים חָשַׁב עַל־הַיְּהוּדִים לְאַבְּדָם וְהִפִּל פּוּר הוּא הַגּוֹרָל לְהֻמָּם וּלְאַבְּדָם: כה וּבְבֹאָהּ לִפְנֵי הַמֶּלֶךְ אָמַר עִם־הַסֵּפֶר יָשׁוּב מַחֲשַׁבְתּוֹ הָרָעָה אֲשֶׁר־חָשַׁב עַל־הַיְּהוּדִים עַל־רֹאשׁוֹ וְתָלוּ אֹתוֹ וְאֶת־בָּנָיו עַל־הָעֵץ:

כו עַל־כֵּן קָרְאוּ לַיָּמִים הָאֵלֶּה פוּרִים עַל־שֵׁם הַפּוּר עַל־כֵּן עַל־כָּל־דִּבְרֵי הָאִגֶּרֶת הַזֹּאת וּמָה־רָאוּ עַל־כָּכָה וּמָה הִגִּיעַ אֲלֵיהֶם: כז קִיְּמוּ °וְקִבְּלוּ הַיְּהוּדִים ׀ עֲלֵיהֶם ׀ וְעַל־זַרְעָם וְעַל כָּל־הַנִּלְוִים עֲלֵיהֶם וְלֹא יַעֲבוֹר לִהְיוֹת עֹשִׂים אֵת שְׁנֵי הַיָּמִים הָאֵלֶּה כִּכְתָבָם וְכִזְמַנָּם בְּכָל־שָׁנָה וְשָׁנָה: כח וְהַיָּמִים הָאֵלֶּה נִזְכָּרִים וְנַעֲשִׂים בְּכָל־דּוֹר וָדוֹר מִשְׁפָּחָה וּמִשְׁפָּחָה מְדִינָה וּמְדִינָה וְעִיר וָעִיר וִימֵי הַפּוּרִים הָאֵלֶּה לֹא יַעַבְרוּ מִתּוֹךְ הַיְּהוּדִים וְזִכְרָם לֹא־יָסוּף מִזַּרְעָם:

°וְקִבֵּל כ'

Different Cities, Different Purims. The Sanhedrin, which was led by Mordechai, wanted to make the holiday of Purim to celebrate the miracle. Since Shushan's miracle was for two days, they made a special Purim for Shushan. But if no other city would have that special Purim, it would be forgotten when Jews no longer lived in Shushan. Therefore the Sages decided that all cities with walls around them — like Shushan — should celebrate Purim on the fifteenth of Adar. The Sages also wanted to give Jerusalem the honor of having that special Purim — but the walls of Jerusalem had been destroyed before the miracle of Purim occurred. So the Sages said that every city that used to have a wall around it in the days of Yehoshua should keep Purim on the fifteenth. In Yehoshua's time, Jerusalem *did* have a wall (*Megillah* 2b).

Esther asked that the Purim story be written in the Tanach. Mordechai became the King's chief officer. He did everything he could to help the Jews, and they loved him.

When Queen Esther, daughter of Avichail, and Mordechai the Jew, wrote with all the power of their high position that the Jews should obey their second letter about Purim. ³⁰To all the Jews — to the hundred and twenty-seven countries of the kingdom of Achashveirosh — Mordechai and Esther sent messages with these words of peace and truth: ³¹That they should always keep these days of Purim on their right dates, just as Mordechai the Jew and Queen Esther had told them to; and as the Jews had accepted upon themselves and their children to keep the fasts and the prayers. ³²Esther requested that these words of Purim should be accepted; and the story was written in the Tanach.

וַתִּכְתֹּב אֶסְתֵּר הַמַּלְכָּה בַת־אֲבִיחַיִל וּמָרְדֳּכַי הַיְּהוּדִי אֶת־כָּל־תֹּקֶף לְקַיֵּם אֵת אִגֶּרֶת הַפֻּרִים הַזֹּאת הַשֵּׁנִית: ל וַיִּשְׁלַח סְפָרִים אֶל־כָּל־הַיְּהוּדִים אֶל־שֶׁבַע וְעֶשְׂרִים וּמֵאָה מְדִינָה מַלְכוּת אֲחַשְׁוֵרוֹשׁ דִּבְרֵי שָׁלוֹם וֶאֱמֶת: לא לְקַיֵּם אֶת־יְמֵי הַפֻּרִים הָאֵלֶּה בִּזְמַנֵּיהֶם כַּאֲשֶׁר קִיַּם עֲלֵיהֶם מָרְדֳּכַי הַיְּהוּדִי וְאֶסְתֵּר הַמַּלְכָּה וְכַאֲשֶׁר קִיְּמוּ עַל־נַפְשָׁם וְעַל־זַרְעָם דִּבְרֵי הַצֹּמוֹת וְזַעֲקָתָם: לב וּמַאֲמַר אֶסְתֵּר קִיַּם דִּבְרֵי הַפֻּרִים הָאֵלֶּה וְנִכְתָּב בַּסֵּפֶר:

י — X

King Achashveirosh made the people on the mainland and the islands pay taxes. ²All his mighty and powerful acts, and the full story of the greatness of Mordechai, whom the King had promoted, are written in the history book of the Kings of Media and Persia. ³For Mordechai the Jew was second in command to King Achashveirosh; he was a great man among the Jews and most of his people liked him. He tried to do good for his nation and to bring peace for all its children.

וַיָּשֶׂם הַמֶּלֶךְ °אֲחַשְׁוֵרוֹשׁ ׀ מַס עַל־הָאָרֶץ וְאִיֵּי הַיָּם: ב וְכָל־מַעֲשֵׂה תָקְפּוֹ וּגְבוּרָתוֹ וּפָרָשַׁת גְּדֻלַּת מָרְדֳּכַי אֲשֶׁר גִּדְּלוֹ הַמֶּלֶךְ הֲלוֹא־הֵם כְּתוּבִים עַל־סֵפֶר דִּבְרֵי הַיָּמִים לְמַלְכֵי מָדַי וּפָרָס: ג כִּי ׀ מָרְדֳּכַי הַיְּהוּדִי מִשְׁנֶה לַמֶּלֶךְ אֲחַשְׁוֵרוֹשׁ וְגָדוֹל לַיְּהוּדִים וְרָצוּי לְרֹב אֶחָיו דֹּרֵשׁ טוֹב לְעַמּוֹ וְדֹבֵר שָׁלוֹם לְכָל־זַרְעוֹ:

°אחשרש כ׳

This blessing is recited if there was a *minyan* at the Megillah reading:

בָּרוּךְ אַתָּה יהוה אֱלֹהֵינוּ מֶלֶךְ הָעוֹלָם, הָרָב אֶת רִיבֵנוּ, וְהַדָּן אֶת דִּינֵנוּ, וְהַנּוֹקֵם אֶת נִקְמָתֵנוּ, וְהַמְשַׁלֵּם גְּמוּל לְכָל אֹיְבֵי נַפְשֵׁנוּ, וְהַנִּפְרָע לָנוּ מִצָּרֵנוּ. בָּרוּךְ אַתָּה יהוה, הַנִּפְרָע לְעַמּוֹ יִשְׂרָאֵל מִכָּל צָרֵיהֶם, הָאֵל הַמּוֹשִׁיעַ. (All — אָמֵן.)

We bless You, Hashem our God, King of the whole world, Who fights for us, judges our claim for us, gets revenge for us, pays back the enemies who want to kill us, and punishes our foes for us. We bless You, Hashem, Who punishes all their foes for the sake of His people Israel; He is the God Who saves.

(All — Amen.)

The following prayer is recited at night after the *Megillah* reading. It is based on the *aleph-beis*, and it tells the story of the *Megillah* in the form of a poem. In the morning we start from שׁוֹשַׁנַּת יַעֲקֹב, *The Rose of Jacob*.

א Hashem stopped the plan of the nations, and He cancelled the ideas of the sly people,

ב When a very bad man, Haman, stood up against us — he did evil on purpose and was a grandchild of Amalek.

ג He bragged about his wealth and he dug his own grave, he was trapped because he wanted to be very important.

ד He thought he could trap the Jews, but he was trapped; he tried to destroy them, but he was quickly destroyed.

ה Haman showed the hatred of his fathers, and he brought back Eisav's hatred of Yaakov against Yaakov's children.

ו Haman didn't remember the mercy of King Shaul, that because of Shaul's pity on Agag, the enemy Haman was born.

ז That evil Haman wanted to kill the tzaddik Mordechai, but that dirty person was caught in the pure man's hands.

ח Mordechai's kindness was stronger than Shaul's sin, but the evil Haman piled sin upon sin.

ט He kept his sneaky ideas a secret, and all he cared about was to do evil.

י He tried to hurt God's holy people, and gave his money to kill their children.

אֲשֶׁר הֵנִיא עֲצַת גּוֹיִם, וַיָּפֶר מַחְשְׁבוֹת עֲרוּמִים.

בְּ קוּם עָלֵינוּ אָדָם רָשָׁע, נֵצֶר זָדוֹן, מִזֶּרַע עֲמָלֵק.

גָּ אָה בְעָשְׁרוֹ, וְכָרָה לוֹ בּוֹר, וּגְדֻלָּתוֹ יָקְשָׁה לוֹ לָכֶד.

דִּ מָּה בְנַפְשׁוֹ לִלְכֹּד, וְנִלְכַּד, בִּקֵּשׁ לְהַשְׁמִיד, וְנִשְׁמַד מְהֵרָה.

הָ מָן הוֹדִיעַ אֵיבַת אֲבוֹתָיו, וְעוֹרֵר שִׂנְאַת אַחִים לַבָּנִים.

וְ לֹא זָכַר רַחֲמֵי שָׁאוּל, כִּי בְחֶמְלָתוֹ עַל אֲגָג נוֹלַד אוֹיֵב.

זָ מַם רָשָׁע לְהַכְרִית צַדִּיק, וְנִלְכַּד טָמֵא, בִּידֵי טָהוֹר.

חֶ סֶד גָּבַר עַל שִׁגְגַת אָב, וְרָשָׁע הוֹסִיף חֵטְא עַל חֲטָאָיו.

טָ מַן בְּלִבּוֹ מַחְשְׁבוֹת עֲרוּמָיו, וַיִּתְמַכֵּר לַעֲשׂוֹת רָעָה.

יָ דוֹ שָׁלַח בִּקְדוֹשֵׁי אֵל, כַּסְפּוֹ נָתַן לְהַכְרִית זִכְרָם.

Eisav, Amalek and Haman. Amalek was a grandson of Eisav, the twin brother of our father Yaakov. Eisav was very jealous of Yaakov and hated him. He taught his little grandson, Amalek to hate Yaakov also. Once Amalek sat on his grandfather's knee and swore that he and his children would always try to kill the Jews. When the Jewish people left Egypt, the Army of Amalek made a sneak attack against them. In the time of King Shaul, too, there was a war between Israel and Amalek. The evil Haman was also from Amalek, and his plan to kill all the Jews was exactly what Eisav and Amalek had hoped for.

Shaul and Agag. In the time of Mordechai's ancestor King Shaul, the prophet Shmuel commanded Shaul to wage a war against Amalek. With *Hashem's* help, Shaul would beat Amalek, and he was to kill every single person and even all the animals. But Shaul did not obey completely. The Jewish people killed *almost* all the people, but Shaul felt sorry for King Agag and did not kill him. While Agag stayed alive, his wife became pregnant and her child was the ancestor of Haman. This means that Haman was alive only because of Shaul's pity on Agag. But that did not stop Haman from hating Mordechai, Shaul's grandchild, and trying to kill Mordechai and his people.

ב When Mordechai saw that the anger began, and Haman's law was given out in Shushan,		בּ רְאוֹת מָרְדֳּכַי, כִּי יָצָא קֶצֶף, וְדָתֵי הָמָן נִתְּנוּ בְשׁוּשָׁן.
ל He dressed in rough sackcloth and clothes of mourning, he ordered everyone to fast and he sat on the ashes.		לָ בַשׁ שַׂק וְקָשַׁר מִסְפֵּד, וְגָזַר צוֹם, וַיֵּשֶׁב עַל הָאֵפֶר.
מ He said, "Who can arise to make up for our mistakes, and to get God to forgive the sins of our fathers?"		מִי זֶה יַעֲמֹד לְכַפֵּר שְׁגָגָה, וְלִמְחֹל חַטַּאת עֲוֹן אֲבוֹתֵינוּ.
נ Like a blossom growing from a date tree, Hadassah stood up to awaken the sleeping Jews.		נֵ ץ פֶּרַח מִלּוּלָב, הֵן הֲדַסָּה עָמְדָה לְעוֹרֵר יְשֵׁנִים.
ס Her servants made Haman hurry, she made him drink the wine that became like poison to him.		סָ רִיסֶיהָ הִבְהִילוּ לְהָמָן, לְהַשְׁקוֹתוֹ יֵין חֲמַת תַּנִּינִים.
ע He stood tall because he was rich, and he fell because he was bad; he put up a gallows, but he was hung on it.		עָ מַד בְּעָשְׁרוֹ, וְנָפַל בְּרִשְׁעוֹ, עָשָׂה לוֹ עֵץ, וְנִתְלָה עָלָיו.
פ All the people in the world open their mouths to praise Hashem, because Haman's lottery became our Purim.		פִּ יהֶם פָּתְחוּ, כָּל יוֹשְׁבֵי תֵבֵל, כִּי פוּר הָמָן נֶהְפַּךְ לְפוּרֵנוּ.
צ The tzaddik Mordechai was saved from the bad man's hand, and the enemy Haman took the tzaddik's place on the gallows.		צַ דִּיק נֶחֱלַץ מִיַּד רָשָׁע, אוֹיֵב נִתַּן תַּחַת נַפְשׁוֹ.
ק The Jews took upon themselves to make the holiday of Purim, and to be happy on it every year.		קִ יְּמוּ עֲלֵיהֶם, לַעֲשׂוֹת פוּרִים, וְלִשְׂמֹחַ בְּכָל שָׁנָה וְשָׁנָה.
ר God, You liked the prayer of Mordechai and Esther, and You hung Haman and his sons on the gallows.		רָ אִיתָ אֶת תְּפִלַּת מָרְדֳּכַי וְאֶסְתֵּר, הָמָן וּבָנָיו עַל הָעֵץ תָּלִיתָ.

This is recited after both *Megillah* readings — night and day.

ש The Rose of Yaakov — the Jewish people — was cheerful and glad, when they all saw Mordechai wearing royal clothes.		שׁוֹשַׁנַּת יַעֲקֹב צָהֲלָה וְשָׂמֵחָה, בִּרְאוֹתָם יַחַד תְּכֵלֶת מָרְדֳּכָי.
ת You, O God, always saved them, and You were their hope in every generation.		תְּ שׁוּעָתָם הָיִיתָ לָנֶצַח, וְתִקְוָתָם בְּכָל דּוֹר וָדוֹר.
You let them know that people who hope for Your help will not be ashamed, and those who depend on You to protect them will never be embarrassed.		לְהוֹדִיעַ, שֶׁכָּל קֹוֶיךָ לֹא יֵבשׁוּ, וְלֹא יִכָּלְמוּ לָנֶצַח כָּל הַחוֹסִים בָּךְ.
A curse on Haman, who tried to destroy me, a blessing on Mordechai, the Jew!		אָרוּר הָמָן, אֲשֶׁר בִּקֵּשׁ לְאַבְּדִי, בָּרוּךְ מָרְדֳּכַי הַיְּהוּדִי.
A curse on Zeresh, the wife of the one who frightened me, a blessing on Esther, who did so much for me! And even Charvonah should be remembered for the good he did.		אֲרוּרָה זֶרֶשׁ, אֵשֶׁת מַפְחִידִי, בְּרוּכָה אֶסְתֵּר בַּעֲדִי, וְגַם חַרְבוֹנָה זָכוּר לַטּוֹב.

To Awaken the Sleeping Jews. Haman's danger came upon the Jews because they had forgotten to pray to *Hashem* and to obey their leader Mordechai. Esther — who was also called Hadassah — made the Jews fast and pray. Most of all, she got them to repent and earn *Hashem's* mercy. That is why the miracle happened.